BARR

Barry Crump wrote his firs
It became an immediate best-seller, as
which followed. His most famous and best-loved New Zealand character is Sam Cash, who features in, Hang On a Minute Mate', Crump's second book. Between them these two books have sold over 400,000 copies and continue to sell at an amazing rate, some thirty years later. Two other Crump books feature Sam Cash 'One of Us' and 'There and Back', both very entertaining and highly successful and due to popular demand have been re-released.

Crump began his working life as a professional hunter, culling deer and pigs in some of the ruggedest country in New Zealand. After the runaway success of his first book, he pursued many diverse activities, including gold-mining, radio talk-back, white-baiting, television presenting, crocodile shooting, acting and numerous others. His face is familiar to all New Zealanders through a series of motor-vehicle commercials which have won world-wide acclaim.

He is listed in the 'Who's Who' as author of no fixed abode. He is currently somewhere in the South Island of New Zealand doing what he fondly calls research. He has contracted one of his books, 'Wild Pork and Watercress' to be made into a full-feature movie. He has also just completed 'The Life and Times of a Good Keen Man', another in the vivid style that has enthralled his readers for three decades. This is the author's own story, something to look forward to, for all Crump fans. This is a fascinating account of the remarkable life of one of New Zealand's truly great characters. As to classifying his occupation, Crump insists that, he always has been, and always will be, a Kiwi bushman, but perhaps these days itinerant scribe would be more appropriate.

BOOKS BY BARRY CRUMP

A Good Keen Man (1960)*
Hang on a Minute Mate (1961)*
One of Us (1962)*
There and Back (1963)*
Gulf (1964) – now titled Crocodile Country*
Scrapwagon (1965)
The Odd Spot of Bother (1967)
No Reference Intended (1968)
Warm Beer and Other Stories (1969)
A Good Keen Girl (1970)
Bastards I Have Met (1971)*
Fred (1972)
Shorty (1980)
Puha Road (1982)*
The Adventures of Sam Cash (1985)
Wild Pork and Watercress (1986)*
Barry Crump Bedtime Yarns (1988)
Bullock Creek (1989)*
The Life and Times of a Good Keen Man (1992)*
Gold and Greenstone (1993)*

*Currently in print 1993

No reference intended to anyone in this book

BARRY CRUMP

PUHA ROAD

BARRY CRUMP ASSOCIATES

'PUHA ROAD'

Published by Barry Crump Associates
P.O. Box 2551, Tauranga, New Zealand.

First edition 1982
Reprints nil
This edition 1993

Distributed by Becket Sterling Ltd.
28 Poland Road, Glenfield, Auckland, New Zealand.

Printed by Australian Print Group, Vic. 3465

ISBN # 0-908968-01-9

Contents

ONE

Muxy's Luck

His real name was Eric Charles Muxworthy, but he was only ever called Muxy except on formal occasions, and I got into more trouble sticking up for him than for anything else during my already trouble-fraught schooldays.

He was an orphan, Muxy was, about a year older than me but in the same form. He didn't have a hell of a lot going for him as far as looks went – fair fluffy hair, plain as a sugar-bag and untidy as a cabbage-tree sticking up out of a flax bush. Prominent front teeth (they used to say he could eat an apple through a tennis racquet, but they weren't *that* bad). Medium height, except that he got around bent forward at the waist, which caused him to have to tilt his head back to see properly, which made him look like a real ning-nong – except that there was something else about him that attracted people.

You could always tell someone who didn't know Muxy very well, they tried to help him. Those who did know him had already given up. Except me, for some reason I never understood. None of the other kids from the orphanage would have much to do with him because he was always getting into trouble, along with anyone who was with him. No one wanted him in their team – he was so accident-prone it was almost impossible to win with him on your side.

And yet despite all this there was something special about Muxy. For one thing he was the most generous person in the school by a mighty margin. He'd jump at the chance to give his bus-money to someone who'd lost theirs, and then he'd have to walk two miles home to the orphanage and get into trouble for being late. You'd give him a pair of sunglasses to hide his black eye and save him being teased about it, and an hour later you'd see someone else wearing them. There was hardly anyone in the school who wasn't indebted to him in some way, otherwise he'd have been dealt-to in the ways of school kids much more than he was.

"It was us, sir!" he'd volunteer helpfully. And everyone involved would shrink down behind their desks, silently cursing the fate that had put Muxy amongst us.

There were always arguments going on about whether he actually attracted trouble, or whether he was just incredibly unlucky. It was said around the school when someone was having a bad run of luck that they had 'A touch of the Muxies'.

Some people said he'd been born under an inauspicious star. Some claimed he did it on purpose. One of the girls used to say he was paying for something terrible he must have done in a previous life. Our old Science Master, bless him, once said that Muxy must have been standing behind the door when all the good luck was being handed out. But whatever they said about him, I was the one who always seemed to end up looking after him, and, as I said, it caused me no end of trouble.

I left school as soon as I was fifteen. Didn't like it there, and for the next few years I knocked around, mainly in the merchant navy, and got into and out of my fair share of trouble and fun.

The funny thing was that every time I came back to Auckland I seemed to run into Muxy again – in the street, at a party, on a bus, in a crowd – and each time I had to help him out of some predicament or other he'd blundered into. Every time it happened I made up my mind that it was never going to happen again. And every time we met I'd be pleased to see him, and suddenly I'd be involved in Muxy's disastrous affairs again.

When I was twenty I came ashore and took up newspaper reporting, which I was pretty good at. Then I got married to a girl I'd known vaguely at school and we settled into paying off a house we had built at Pakuranga.

I didn't get on any better at marriage than I had at school. My wife was always pushing me to 'make something of myself' and I was always finding it hard enough to stick at the reporting jobs I got as it was. She claimed I drank too much and I happened to know it was barely enough.

Eventually we found ourselves the constantly-bickering parents of a four-year-old daughter. We couldn't talk to one another without it becoming an argument. It wasn't doing our daughter any more good than it was doing us. I left one morning in April, by mutual agreement, and never went back there.

I heard a few weeks later that my wife had moved into a flat and put the house up for sale, but I was busy with other things by this time and didn't care what she did. I'd given up trying to make it to the top, I was staying at the bottom where it wasn't such a hassle.

Some of my friends tried to persuade me to pull my socks up, but I liked my socks the way they were, and set about catching up on all the good times I'd missed out on while I was married.

There'd be plenty of time for the pulling up of any socks that needed it later on, I reckoned.

Three years later I was a wreck. An alcoholic, they claimed, and finally I was forced to agree that they could be right. I couldn't get work any more because I couldn't be relied on to meet a deadline. With thousands unemployed nobody had to put up with a slack journalist. I had two choices – go into an institution or pull up those socks they'd been warning me about. I decided to have a go at the sock one.

I contacted Alcoholics Anonymous and they left me in no doubt that I was a fully paid-up alcoholic – I'd spent everything on it.

Without A.A. I wouldn't have known where to start; with them, there was no doubt. I spent three months at Hanmer Springs, drying out, and then came back to Auckland and got a furnished flat in Parnell, and part-time work writing freelance articles for a couple of sporting weekly papers.

Keeping out of the pubs and away from all my old drinking buddies made me a suspicious character in the eyes of my landlady, Mrs Hollows. Flats were almost as hard to get as jobs, at this stage, and landladies were taking on a new authority. Mine was given to hinting that she didn't have to put up with anything she didn't happen to like.

I'd been in that flat about six months, and one day as I was leaving my lawyer's office with my *Decree Absolute* papers in my pocket I saw some people clustered around someone who'd caught his hand in the old-fashioned lift doors in the foyer of the building. A nurse was there telling them it was probably only bruised.

"Muxy!" I called out.

"Well I never," he said. "It's Gavin Midwinter!"

When we were on our own out on the street I asked him, "How're things with you, Muxy?"

"Terrific," he grinned, still nursing his injured hand.

I didn't believe him. He had a reasonably good suit on, but it was in bad condition. He'd been sleeping in it, if I knew Muxy.

"Had a feed lately?" I asked him.

"Well – no. I was expecting to get some money from . . ."

"Come on," I grabbed him by the arm and we settled into the first coffee bar we came to. Muxy ate everything in sight while he filled me in on some of his more recent adventures between mouthfuls.

He hadn't changed much in the two years or so since I'd last seen him – it was all bad news. Up until a month before, he'd been working in a travel-agency, but a girl he'd met there was transferred to Hastings before she'd got to know him properly. Muxy had started sending messages to her on their machine and they caught him at it one day and gave him the sack. Before that he was a trucker's off-sider, for one week. Before that he'd lasted a few days with the railways. And before that he'd been on a maintenance gang, painting around the wharves for the Harbour Board, but they'd got sick of fishing him out of the drink and sent him packing before he got drowned. And so on, right back to the time he was standing behind the door when all the good luck was being handed out.

Muxy was about twenty-eight years old at this stage. He couldn't be certain because when he'd tried to get a copy of his Birth Certificate they found out that his birth hadn't been registered properly. There was a hell of a rigmarole to go through to put it right and Muxy just wasn't up to it.

I guessed Mrs Hollows could handle Muxy staying with me for a while, just till he got on his feet again. There was a warning voice in my head behind my right ear saying 'Don't do it! Don't do it!' but what could a bloke do? An old acquaintance having a bad trot and down on his luck.

I still shouldn't have done it. We didn't even make it home before it started. Muxy was sitting with his hand on the door handle of my sixty-seven Dodge and when we went around a busy corner he leaned on it. The door flew open and suddenly Muxy was bowling up the road. I pulled up as quick as it was safe and Muxy stood up just in time to get sent flying again by a girl who overtook us on a trail bike. It was unreal! One moment we were driving peacefully home to the flat, and the next my passenger was being knocked down by a motorbike right in front of me!

We got it sorted out by giving the girl a few bucks for a new blinker-light glass and a pair of pantyhose. Muxy reckoned he wasn't hurt, but he was limping badly on one hip, his suit was ruined, his lip was split, his nose was skinned and he appeared to have re-hurt the hand he'd got caught in the lift. It still didn't straighten out his grin, though. He'd obviously had it worse than this plenty of times. As always, he picked himself up, brushed himself down, stuck the grin back on his dial and limped off in the direction of the next disaster.

I was still more shaken than Muxy when we arrived home, where Muxy immediately got off-side with Mrs Hollows. He couldn't have done it worse if he'd deliberately set out to antagonise her. For a start his appearance was against him. Hair all over the place, nearly all the elbows and knees ripped out of his suit, blood smeared around his face. I'm not fussy, but his shirt – well it was filthy. He couldn't stand up straight and one hand was being kept out of sight as though he was hiding something behind his back. Even before he spoke I could tell that Muxy wasn't going to be exactly number one on Mrs H's chart.

He cheerfully informed her that he'd been out of work for quite a while and would be staying with me until he got on his feet again. Then he went on to explain what a good thing it was that I'd come along when I did, because he didn't have a red cent to his name. He rounded off the whole dismal performance by confiding to her that he was 'heavily in debt', whereupon I dragged him away up the stairs before she threw us out onto the street there and then.

"Nice lady," observed Muxy as I was getting the flat door open.

"She's pretty strong on blokes having steady jobs and money in the bank," I told him.

"Yes," he agreed. "Nice lady."

I let the matter drop for the time being and made us a mug of coffee.

"How much money do you owe, Muxy?" I asked him.

"Sixteen dollars and eighty-five cents. It's a big worry."

"Sixteen bucks?"

"Yes, it's what I've got left to pay on this suit, actually. I've had warning letters."

I wrote out a cheque for the amount and we put it in an envelope and found the address among the mess in Muxy's memory. Then I made him have a bath, a shave, some of my clothes, another mug of coffee and a sleeping bag on the sofa. We could take it from there in the morning. And that's how it all more or less started.

Next morning we found some possible jobs for him in the newspaper. I gave him a few dollars and sent him off, still limping but eager as a pup, to find a new career. That afternoon he arrived back, no luck. That is no good luck. There was a superabundance of the other kind.

Although I'd known Muxy for years I'd never lived this close to him before and I was in for a rude awakening. I'll have to mention some of the bad luck he had or you'd never be able to believe how it was.

The first place he'd tried he actually got the job, but when they sent him down to start work, the foreman had worked with Muxy once before on a different job and he kicked up such a stink that they had to let Muxy go with a day's pay and an apology. By this time it was late in the morning and everywhere else he tried the job was either already taken or something went drastically wrong during the interview.

That's how it went for the next few weeks. We'd get up in the morning, go through the 'Situations Vacant', and send Muxy off with instructions and advice and directions and a wan 'Good

Luck'. And every day he came home with stories of such devastating bad luck that at times he had me doubting my sanity.

When he did get a job he couldn't seem to hang onto it for long enough to get paid. For example he was actually taken on by the Power Board for a while. One morning and part of an afternoon to be exact. He made it through the morning all right, but got the afternoon off to a bad start by sitting on the foreman's lunch. It can't have been too smooth a morning because the foreman threw his squashed lunch at Muxy. I'd have believed the foreman if he'd claimed to have had an exasperating morning with his new labourer.

Once these things start they just seem to keep on happening, especially with Muxy, and just as the gang truck was pulling up at their first job after lunch, Muxy somehow fell off the back and landed on the top of his head on the concrete. He got up and climbed back onto the truck okay, but he didn't seem to be able to understand that they'd just arrived there. He thought it was time to go home, so eventually they brought him there.

He arrived in the Power Board ute with the foreman, who hinted that Muxy might be better suited to any other occupation than in his gang. It was concussion, Muxy reckoned, nothing to worry about, he'd had it plenty of times. I kept a close eye on him for a few days after that but he seemed to be okay and I soon forgot about the Power Board adventure in the welter of incredible bad luck that continued to overtake poor, cheerful, exasperating Muxy.

Every now and again Muxy's travels took him near somewhere he'd stayed in the past, and he often picked up some of the gear he'd left there. It was accumulating in the flat at a disquieting rate. One day Mrs Hollows met him trying to get a big old one-piece surfcasting rod round the corner and up the stairs.

"Mr Muxworth!" she said in a voice that brought me out of the flat running. "What on earth are you doing with that big stick in here?"

"It's my surfcaster," explained Muxy. "I've just picked it up. Not bad, eh!"

"You can't bring that in here," she said in her worst voice. "You'll break something!"

I went down and helped him get it up the stairs and round the corner into the flat.

"Have you ever caught anything with it, Muxy?" I asked him.

"Too right! I'm real good at it, I'll show you one day."

It wasn't easy to equate Muxy with surfcasting. He would have been drowned, or dragged out to sea or something.

"Sure," I said. "In the meantime we'd better just prop it across the wall behind the sofa here."

That afternoon Muxy went off to try for a job with a cleaning firm. He was running a bit early so he nipped into a department store to use the toilet, and got locked in the building when everybody left for the day. Someone going up the footpath after the movies that night finally spotted Muxy banging and waving behind the big glass doors of the store and told a couple of policemen about him. It was one o'clock in the morning by the time they'd got everything together to let Muxy out.

The police took him down to Central and grilled him trying to find out why the hell he hadn't picked up one of the dozens of telephones in the store and rung their afterhours number. But Muxy stuck to his original story, that he didn't think of it (he never did trust telephones). When they had nothing left to do but believe him, they brought him home at three-thirty in the morning, in a police car. They woke up Mrs Hollows and warned her to keep an eye on him, which was not calculated to warm the cockles of Mrs H's unforgiving heart. I heard it from the landing.

"This person is not my son, officer," she informed them primly. "He is a temporary guest of one of my tenants who I don't expect will be staying here for very much longer."

While she was busy with the policeman, Muxy ducked up the stairs and I shoved him into the flat and closed the door behind us.

"What the hell's happened?" I said.

He told me.

And I'd been thinking his luck must have changed and he'd got the cleaning job. Silly of me, eh!

Next morning when Muxy had gone off job-hunting, Mrs Hollows headed me off in the hallway and enquired when we might expect 'that Mr Muxworth' to get on his feet.

"He was brought home by the police just before daylight this morning, you know, Mr Midwinter."

"Yes, but I understand it was nothing Muxy did wrong," I said.

"When do you think he'll be leaving?" she insisted.

"Any old day now, Mrs Hollows," I told her cheerfully.

"Do you think you could promise to have him out of your flat by the end of the week?" she re-insisted.

"Oh I should think so, Mrs H," I assured her.

"All right," she said. "The end of the week then."

"Unless of course something goes wrong," I said. "You can never tell about some of these things."

"That man *makes* things go wrong," she said. "I don't care what you say, there's something unlucky about him. He's probably one of those Scorpios, if you ask me, and the sooner he's out of this house the happier I'll be." And she marched off having said rather more than she'd intended.

She was also partly influenced by the fact that she could raise the rent on the flat considerably to a new tenant by this time. We were costing her money. The writing was on the wall, the skids were under us. It was only a matter of time before we were out of there.

I didn't say anything to Muxy about it. He thought Mrs Hollows liked him as much as he liked her, and I didn't want to disillusion him unnecessarily. That day he'd missed out on three jobs, but he had found a hundred and forty-five dollars in a folder on the footpath. He seemed to think the best thing to do with it was wait for the owner to advertise and get the reward.

And there it was in the paper next morning, no mistake, the

right amount, the right place, reward offered!

Now this looked like a change of luck to me, and I was all for it. I lent Muxy some of my good clothes to go and collect his reward and then apply for a job as a messenger for Radio New Zealand. He arrived back a couple of hours later with grease all over my good trousers from helping a lady whose chain had come off her bike, no job, and two dollars-fifty left of the twenty-dollar reward he'd been given.

He could be pretty damn indiscreet at times, Muxy. One evening I had a visit from a lady I was friendly with. I introduced her to Muxy and the very first thing he said to her was, "Oh, you must be the Judith who's been trying to hook Gavin! Pleased to meet you!"

She left without taking her coat off.

"What the hell did you want to go and say that for?" I said to Muxy when she'd gone.

"Say what?" He really didn't know!

"Tell Judith I reckoned she was trying to hook me?" I said.

"Hadn't you told her you reckoned that?"

"No I bloody hadn't!"

"Well no wonder you're upset."

"What do you mean, no wonder I'm upset?"

"You should always say things like that to the person concerned first," he admonished me. "You always get into trouble by telling the wrong people things like that."

"Well I'll make good and bloody sure I don't tell you anything like that in future."

"That's nice. I don't like knowing things I can't talk about." He was grinning again, so I went to bed.

Not long after that Muxy got a job with a tar-sealing outfit. He lasted three days. They brought him home on the fourth morning with tar-burns on his legs and the tops of his feet. They'd patched him up and he reckoned he'd had it worse and would be right again in a day or two. It was a relief in a way, because even Muxy could see by this time that a bloke with his record was no good working around hot tar and heavy traffic.

I wasn't getting much work done with Muxy lying around injured half the time, and out somewhere the other half, worrying me about what condition he was going to come home in. It couldn't go on happening indefinitely, surely.

"I don't think I've ever seen such a rotten run of luck as you're having just lately," I said to him one morning.

"I don't believe in luck," he said.

"Can't say I blame you."

"No, I mean if you believe in good luck you have to believe in bad luck as well."

"That'd be right," I agreed.

"Well the same things are going to happen to you whether you think it's good luck or bad luck."

"Maybe," I conceded.

"Then what's the point of worrying about whether things that happen are good or bad luck?"

"You're telling the story."

"Well you seem to think I have had bad luck all the time."

"That's putting it mildly."

"I don't think I'm unlucky at all," he said.

"Look," I said, suddenly losing patience with him. "You've got no place of your own to live, hardly any clothes, no money and you haven't had a steady job for months. You've tried for dozens of jobs in the last few weeks and missed out on every one of them because of bad luck. In fact you're bloody lucky you ran into me, or you'd be . . ." He was grinning at me.

"Bloody lucky," he agreed.

He was right up to a point, he always was, but his good luck or whatever it was, was running me both ragged and broke.

"I don't suppose you've got any money left?" I said.

"No, as a matter of fact I haven't."

"Hell, man. You must be giving money to people!"

"I do."

"Well cut it out, will you. We need money too, you know."

"Oh I never give it to anyone who's got more than us," he explained seriously. "They've usually got none at all."

"Well just take it easy, will you. We haven't got very much of the stuff left." And I handed him another ten bucks to give to the blokes outside the pubs. He took it as though he was doing me a favour by distributing my money among the hard-up for me.

That was the day Mrs Hollows pulled me aside and confided that she needed us out of the flat by Monday week because she was having the whole top floor renovated. I got the impression that she was prepared to dismantle the building and re-assemble it when we were gone. I told her we'd be out by Monday week and went for a drive in the Dodge to think.

It wasn't a good time to have to find another flat. Two of my articles had been returned by the papers and I'd altered them around and re-submitted them, and they'd come back again. I had just over three hundred dollars left in the bank and they owed me for three other stories. I was worth maybe five hundred bucks altogether and the car needed a bit of work done on it.

And then of course there was Muxy. I'd ended up feeling responsible for him again, only this time I seemed to be stuck with him. Not that he wasn't a decent sort, and in between disasters he could be great value, but there'd been disturbingly little time between disasters lately. I could have quite easily got away from him if I'd wanted to, but when it came to taking my mind off my own problems Muxy was irreplaceable.

I hadn't done anything about getting us another flat by the time our notice was up, so we jammed our gear into the Dodge, with Muxy's surfcasting rod tied from bumper to bumper over the roof, and hunted around the accommodation agencies until we found a flat at Greenlane for sixty-five dollars a week. It was a miserable little joint; grey, green and poky, but we hoped it was only temporary.

Instead of Muxy having got on his feet we were now both out of work. We'd agreed it was a waste of time to register for the dole. It was six months before you could get your first payment anyway. We were going to need money a lot sooner than that. Jobs were becoming harder to get all the time, especially in and around the city, but we had the Dodge. We could try for work further out of town.

Actually I had the ridiculous notion that Muxy'd be less likely to run into serious trouble or bad luck in a more rural situation. I'm still humbly grateful that I didn't know how wrong I was.

I'd been through a few hectic times during four and a half years in the merchant navy, but what I was yet to go through with Muxy made my navy experience as tame to look back on as a knitting seminar.

TWO

The Bottom Of The Barrel

It wasn't easy at first. It wasn't easy at any time, if it comes to that, but at first it was extra hard to make a decision. For instance I'd think of putting in a tender for a contract to paint a building somewhere, (a seaman can always sling a paint brush), but was it safe to take Muxy up a twenty-foot ladder with a gallon of paint? For that matter, was it safe to take him anywhere? Was it safe to leave him on his own? Was it safe to stand near him? Alas – no!

After a while I came to the conclusion that there was no point in worrying about it, and didn't let it influence me any more than I could help. After all, Muxy was tough, and a bloke with his track-record had to be really very lucky to be still running around more or less in one piece. There was no doubt that he'd taken a terrific amount of punishment, even in the bit of time I'd actually been there to see it, but why should I worry about it more than he did? Here he was, sitting beside me in the car, as though he didn't have a care in the world, prattling on about all the things people had been giving him lately. The Dodge was crammed with it.

"What the hell makes people give you all this stuff, Muxy?" I asked him, shaking my head at the thought of it.

"It's because I give things away," he said.

"Then how come you've got so much of it?"

"Because when you give things away you get back more than you give. It gets ahead of you sometimes."

"Doesn't work that way with me, I'm afraid."

"Sure it does, it's the same for everyone."

"Then how come everyone isn't running around giving stuff away?"

"Because they don't see how it works," he explained. "They lend things."

"What's wrong with lending things?" I wanted to know.

"Nothing, but it's not the same as giving things."

"We're not all as generous as you, which is probably just as well, otherwise we'd all be running around giving things to each other and nobody'd get any work done."

"Oh I'm not generous," he denied, "I only give things to people because I like doing it. It also happens to be the best way to get true wealth."

"It would be if it worked."

"But it does work!"

"Prove it."

"What do you think all this is?" he asked, waving at the stuff piled to the roof in the back seat.

"True wealth?" I asked, looking across at him.

In spite of Muxy's objections I made us sell off some of our true wealth to an auction mart for eighty dollars. A transistor radio, a primus stove, a folding deckchair, a hanging pot plant and a leather-bound set of classical novels.

"Someone might have needed some of that stuff," he protested.

"Cut it out, Muxy. We needed to get a bit of the weight off the wagon, and the money we got for it can go towards helping the poor."

"The poor? What poor?"

"Us. We're going to run out of money real soon unless we get some kind of work."

"The idea of going broke worries you, doesn't it Gav."

"Yeah, why not? Doesn't it worry you?"

"I'd be worried all the time if that worried me," he grinned.

"Well I haven't got a mug like me to look after me," I said. "I usually have to work for a living."

"Depends how you look at it, Gav."

"Sure does."

We were getting uncomfortably short of money by the time we landed the job on a stud-cattle farm out at Waiuku, living in comfortable quarters and doing casual labour for a hundred bucks a week each and our keep.

For the first few days Muxy and I were working together, stacking timber and cleaning up around a big barn they had there, and I managed to head off most of the disasters and cover up the rest. On the fourth day they separated us and Muxy lasted less than an hour. They were unloading some fencing material off a truck. A roll of barbed wire rolled off the top of the load when they let the ropes go, and Muxy didn't know how heavy it was. In fact he'd never seen a roll of three-inch hog-barb before. He tried to catch it for them. And it landed in his arms and sent him sprawling, with severe lacerations of the arms, chest and chin. I was only grateful I didn't see it happen. The boss was puzzled but sympathetic about it and Muxy was as right as rain in a week, though he had a scar on his chin for the rest of his life as a souvenir.

In fact the boss didn't wake up to us until we'd been there nearly a month. Muxy backed the tractor through some rails and into the big goldfish pond they had in the front garden, and all the strange events of the past few weeks fell into place for the boss. In what I thought was rather indecent haste, he gave us a week's pay in lieu of notice and encouraged us to try and be gone by the time his wife came home at three o'clock. It's a bit eerie to be not wanted around so urgently and obviously. Muxy was used to it and it didn't seem to worry him more than anything else did, but I wasn't used to being treated like that and found I had a tendency to get indignant about it. We were halfway back to town before I settled down from the experience.

Our new residence turned out to be half a small house at St Heliers; old, blue, green and forty dollars a week, with a forty-dollar bond in case we damaged anything or left without giving notice.

It's hardly worth mentioning the job we got on the deer farm at Kaipara, except that we lost the bond on the flat in our hurry to get out there and secure what sounded like an interesting job. We needn't have hurried, as it turned out. The very first afternoon we were there Muxy got cornered by a stag he'd been trying to make friends with and he had to be dragged out under the fence just in time.

"I can't understand it," the bloke said. "That animal's never behaved like that before. The kids reared him on a bottle!"

"Don't worry about it, Len," I told him. "Muxy gets a bit unlucky with certain animals. It probably won't happen with anyone else."

He was a real nice bloke, Len. He let Muxy work around the yard for a week or so, because he was too nervous to get out of the Land Rover when we were working around the deer, but it wasn't worth him paying two men for what he was getting out of it. He wasn't doing that well. Muxy and I had a talk about it one night and decided to tell Len we wanted to drop the deal. It's no good working for anyone under those circumstances, it couldn't last.

Len must have been meditating on the same subject because he saw our point at once when we made mention of it at breakfast next morning. He was silent for a moment, then he said, "I'll give you a few bucks for your trouble."

"No, thanks all the same," we told him. "We're just sorry it didn't work out."

"Yeah, well, so am I. Good luck to you both, anyway."

"Thanks, mate."

That was one of our less troublesome departures. It depended on how good they were at concealing their relief.

We drove back into town and hunted around until we found a poky little yellow and green flat in Mt Eden, from where we continued our search for congenial employment.

It wasn't as easy to get jobs for two men as it might have been to get them singly, and jobs were getting more like hens' teeth all the time, scarce. The only thing to do was take our chances and hope something a little more permanent turned up before we ran out of money altogether.

We could have got a job cutting back roadsides for the Waterworks Department up in the Waitakeres, but the idea of Muxy swinging a slasher had an unpleasant edge to it and I shied off the proposition. And not long after that it looked for a while as though our luck had changed. A farmer out at Pukekohe accepted the price we offered in reply to his ad for contractors to clear some willow trees away from a drain. Either we'd underquoted or we were lucky. There was only one way to find out.

It cost us the fifty-dollar bond we'd paid on the flat, and almost all the rest of our money for a second-hand chainsaw and other gear we needed, but we had to have a go at it. We had the use of a cottage near the job and it started off quite well. No way was I going to let Muxy handle the chainsaw, but he was happier to throw the cut-up branches into heaps for burning anyway.

The trunks of the trees were a problem at first, and then we had another stroke of luck! A bloke passing in a car stopped and had a look at the willow trunks we'd been wondering what to do with. He was an official of the A&P Society, and they needed a hundred willow blocks for the woodchopping championships. He offered us five dollars a block to cut them to length and stack them on the bank beside the road to be picked up by the carrier.

The day we helped them load the blocks on a truck they handed me an envelope with a cheque for five hundred dollars in it. I was suspicious of all this good luck with Muxy around. I hadn't seen anything so lucky happen so close to him before.

It was okay. Our luck held for three weeks, long enough for us to finish the contract and collect the cheque. The farmer even bought the chainsaw off us.

We had thirteen hundred dollars worth of cheques in our possession. I was cautious; something had to happen to that money, or Muxy's luck had changed. He hadn't injured himself seriously during the whole tricky job, and he hadn't given anything away for so long I was beginning to risk hoping a little.

When we got back to Auckland Muxy wanted to go to the bank and cash our cheques because he'd never handled that much money before. And I went and let him. I was chasing around after a new oil filter for the Dodge and I had two numbers to ring for possible flats. So I let him. No excuse, really.

He was a bit late meeting me back at the car, and we drove out to Birkenhead to have a look at a flat I'd rung up about.

"Let me get this straight," I said. "You're trying to tell me that on the way back from the bank you bought a piano for a Samoan girl for two hundred and eighty dollars of our willow contract money?"

It was so outrageous I was beyond anger. He was so obviously guilty of having done a demonstrably-bad thing that I might even be able to use it to make him promise to cut it out altogether. But he didn't seem to be very guilty about it at all. He was like a pup that had found some exciting rotten stuff and rolled in it and come bouncing back to share the fragrance with you.

"No," he patiently explained. "I only paid it off for her. They'd repossessed it, actually. They were taking it out of a van into the shop and she was trying to stop them when I came along. I had to give them an extra thirty dollars to take it back to her place. Lucky I happened along when I did eh!"

"Thought you didn't believe in luck?" I reminded him.

"I bet that Samoan girl does right now," he grinned. "She was pretty, Gav!"

"Where's the rest of the money?"

"Right here."

"Thanks," I said, holding out my hand.

"What's the matter? Don't you trust me?"

"No," I said, tucking the roll into my pocket. "I don't trust you. You'd give it away quicker than we could make it. You'd have us broke again in no time."

"Hardly," he said. "You'd never go broke giving that much of your money to someone in trouble. You only go broke when you try to hang onto your money and fail."

"That's my problem exactly," I said. "Let's do it my way till we see what we get back on our investment, shall we? In the meantime, if you want to give anyone any money, ask me first. Okay?"

It was going to be a while before I trusted him after that little episode.

We took the Birkenhead flat. Grey, blue, cream and musty. Eighty bucks bond against damage or defection. And three weeks later we blew the bond in our hurry to get to a job on a donkey farm at Hunua.

We thought we were lucky at first. Fred Clurk was this bloke's name. We met him outside Papakura and followed his Land Rover to his place on a windswept ridge, miles up a side road. I looked around. Everything I saw was unfinished. The house had never been completed; the sheds had never been painted; the fences had anywhere from none to seven wires on them; the garden had been rotary-hoed but never planted; the driveway had been boxed but never concreted, even the letterbox was sitting on the ground beside its post.

His forty-odd acres ran down one side of the ridge to a swamp full of blackberries and rubbish at the bottom, with the unfinished house at the top near the road. He had about a dozen fluffy moulting donkeys wandering around. He wanted to go in for breeding mules, he told us, and needed a few paddocks fenced-off so he could organise his stock better.

Apparently Fred's wife and two kids were running some kind of shop in town and came out to the farm in the holidays sometimes. We were to sleep in a caravan parked on half-flat tyres beside the house and eat with Fred in the house.

All this sounded fair enough, but I tell you, Fred Clurk and Muxy were a devastating combination. They were both dreamers, both dithery; both very courteous, both financially irresponsible, both accident-prone, and both unconcerned about it. If they hadn't looked different it wouldn't have mattered which of them you had with you.

Our first day working for Fred turned out to be fairly typical. We got up in the morning and went over to the house for breakfast. Fred knocked over some brooms when he was letting us in, Muxy dived to pick them up, Fred's old black Labrador mistook Muxy's intentions and bit him on the leg. Then it dived off the porch when Fred took a swipe at it, and smashed a glass flagon on the concrete path. Fred, all sympathy, hurried Muxy into the bathroom to wash the bite with disinfectant. While they were in there I cleaned up the broken glass, and while I was doing that a pan of dripping Fred had left on the stove caught fire. I smothered it with the mat off the floor. By the look of the scorch-marks on the wall it had happened at least twice before. Muxy and Fred came back into the kitchen, where Muxy immediately put his hand on the hot part of the stove. Fred rousted out a tin of ointment and tore up an old pillowcase to bandage Muxy's burn with. I went into the bathroom just in time to see the water spilling over the top of the basin. They'd left the plug in and the tap running. When I got back to the kitchen Muxy and Fred were scraping up sugar off the floor. One of them had dropped the sugar-tin and it had gone everywhere.

I plugged in a jug of water and started making toast. Only one side of the toaster worked, but that was nothing, the jug didn't work at all. It had been burnt-out long ago.

We boiled a pot of water on the one element left working on the stove and made a cup of tea, only Fred forgot to empty the teapot before he made the fresh brew, and we had both fresh tea and stewed tea in the same cup, with toast and cheese.

That was breakfast. We'd got up at seven-thirty and it was ten o'clock by the time we'd done the washing up and left the house.

Out on the job we addressed ourselves to the erection of a hundred-metre stretch of fence that had been started on some time in the past and never finished. Muxy took the wire up to the other end. Fred fixed the wire-strainers at this end and between them they then went and brought Muxy's wire back. I started digging post holes while Muxy found some cobweb for a cut on Fred's thumb.

Then they went up to the house to have a look for a pair of good boots Fred thought just might fit Muxy. They were gone about two hours, and when they returned they brought me a billy of tea. They got it all the way down to the job before they spilled it. They'd also brought me some sandwiches which they'd dropped in the dirt getting through the gate and given to the donkeys and the dog. They both entreated me to let them go back and do it again, but I wouldn't let them. I couldnt' bear it.

During what was left of the afternoon Fred put a stay in the wrong side of a strainer while Muxy cut a hundred-yard stretch of high-tensile wire six feet too short. He hadn't allowed for a dip the fence had to go through. We tied in an extra length of wire, and next time he allowed plenty for the dip, but cut it too short again.

By the time all this had been accomplished it was time to knock off. On the way up to the house Fred saw one of his donkeys out on the road, so he told us to go ahead and get dinner started, while he went and brought the donkey back.

We cooked dinner, ate it, washed up, watched television for a couple of hours, ate Fred's dinner and cooked him some sausages and eggs and left them in the oven, and went to bed about eleven o'clock.

We heard Fred arrive home about half past eleven. Apparently his donkey had trotted around in front of him all over the district before it got bored and let him catch it. They were like that, Fred's donkeys. They kicked him, bit him, bucked him off – they had him conned!

It could have been argued that it had been our first day on the job and we would probably settle into a rhythm of work after that, but no, it went on happening. The next morning Muxy and I were sitting on the steps in the sun, watching Fred come back up the hill from feeding a donkey that was off-colour. Fred must have wanted a block of wood for something because he wandered over and kicked one out from behind the wheel of a horse-float, which as he strolled away with his block of wood, trundled slowly backwards down the hill and lodged halfway through one of the few decent fences on the place. Fred looked around when he heard the crash, gazed at it for a while, and then came on up to the house. "Forgot about that," he said.

And we had to spend the rest of the day dragging the horse-float back up the hill and fixing the broken fence.

I lasted it out for ten days. By this time the general atmosphere, the infirmity of purpose, was starting to affect me. One night, after picking our way through a charred meal of braised steak and onions and washing it down with tepid milky tea, I told them I couldn't stay there.

They didn't want to hear it. Look at all the work we've got done, they said.

"Two good men could have done all that in a morning," I said. "A fencing contractor would charge you less to do the whole job in two weeks than you'd end up paying us to muddle along the way we are."

The next morning Muxy and Fred were still prepared to muddle along the way we were, so I chucked my gear into the Dodge and backed around, opened the passenger's door for Muxy and his gear when he came running out, and drove away from Fred and his donkey farm. Some things just have to be done. I'd been getting afraid to wake up in the morning.

A couple of days later we moved into a flat in an old house in Sandringham, apricot and cream. Forty-five bucks deposit.

Because of Muxy's imperviousness to criticism or praise, his almost-constant cheerfulness; his unbelievable bad luck; his touching consideration for other people; that grin of his; his willingness to be of assistance; the carloads of stuff he unwittingly inspired people to give us; his inability to see anything wrong with anybody, and his insistence that I was his best friend and the only person who'd ever understood him, by the end of another two months we were getting close to being broke again and I'd had a gutsful of trying to do something with him. We were driving back to town after failing to impress the boss of a pruning gang in the Silverdale forestry.

The only potential material use Muxy was to us was that people were generous towards him, but he didn't give their generosity a chance to help us. Getting him to sell anything that had been given to him as a gift was downright disheartening. At one stage I persuaded him to sell an electric toaster an old lady he'd mowed a lawn for had given him. He sold the toaster for eight dollars, which was good, and then he gave away ten dollars on his way back to the car, which was not so good.

"Look, Muxy," I said, "I've been thinking."

"What about?"

"You."

"Me?"

"Yes, you."

"What about me?"

"You're bloody impossible, that's what."

"In what way?"

"In every way. I can't do a thing with you, so I've decided to give up trying."

"That's nice to know," he said warmly.

"What do you mean, nice to know?"

"I always feel sorry for people who try to do something with me," he said. "I'd change to please them, if I could, but I just can't. I'm made the way I am and I seem to be the only one who doesn't mind the way I am."

"Garn!" I ruffled his hair for him. "There's more to it than that though, Muxy."

"What?"

"Well, I can't go on bumming around like this. It's got to end pretty soon anyway. I'm a journalist, and I have to settle down somewhere so I can concentrate on making a living."

"Can't you do both?"

"How do you mean?"

"Can't you write your articles in between jobs? It doesn't matter when you write them does it?"

"Out of the question," I snapped. "It's impossible."

"Are you sure you just haven't thought about it before?" he said.

"Quite bloody sure, thanks."

Every time I got hacked-off with Muxy something would happen, like him having to use me as his next-of-kin on a form he was filling out, to remind me I was the only one he had in the world, and I'd end up admiring him for having the guts to risk annoying me in the first place. He'd never found out if he had a single relative, alive or dead, except that the orphanage people had told him that he'd been put up for adoption as a baby and had never been lucky enough to catch the eye of the right prospective parents. That'd be Muxy.

"Doesn't it ever worry you, not having any family or relatives or that?" I'd asked him one day.

"I've got you," he said. "I never had any other family."

"Yes, but . . ." I didn't know how to say it.

"But what?"

"Nothing. It doesn't matter."

It was a hell of a responsibility to lay on a man, though.

I started on the first article the next afternoon, and wrote two of them in two and a half hours. It didn't solve our immediate problem – money – but it was a bit more comfortable knowing we probably had some coming to us later on. Besides that it did me good; put me in a better frame of mind.

Not that it did much to hinder our inexorable advance towards the bottom of the barrel. It seemed to me that the Chief Justice's pay would have failed to keep pace with Muxy's unique combination of hair-raising generosity and outrageous bad luck.

THREE

The Crest Of The Wave

If Muxy's bad luck was staggering in its scope and persistence, his good luck, when it finally did arrive, was absolutely amazing. And it couldn't have come at a better time, except maybe a bit sooner.

After five utterly disastrous days trying to bluff a drainage contractor at Maramarua that we knew what we were doing, we were lucky to have got away without having to pay for any of the damage caused when a Hitachi digger fell somehow sideways into the swamp. It had been our last hope, that job, and it had fallen more than flat. We'd left it too late to even register for the dole in time to save us.

We'd limped into Auckland in the middle of the night and dozed in the Dodge until the shops opened. I sold the socket-set and pawned my typewriter and brought our finances up from nearly nothing to twenty-one dollars. We'd spent ten on a meal, Muxy lost five dollars somewhere between the cafe and the car, and we'd just put six dollars and thirty-seven cents worth of gas in the car.

So this was it, the bottom of the barrel. The thing I'd been staving off and planning against with Muxy for more than seven months had finally happened. We were broke.

It was a relief. We were truly in the hands of whatever fate had in store for us.

I could stop worrying now and be like Muxy. The Dodge had deteriorated so badly we had to park it on a slope to make sure it started next time.

The left front tyre had no tread left on it and was due to blow any time, and the spare was flat and no one would risk putting another boot in it for us. Also, the Dodge had been overloaded for so long that the rear springs were sagging and something was scraping every time we went over a bump.

The only decent thing to do was get out of town before we came undone completely and wound up in the hands of the police, or some other benevolent authority.

I decided to try and get over to Devonport and hope my brother-in-law wasn't home, so I could snip my sister for a few bucks to get us clear of the city. And as we drove onto the Harbour Bridge I suddenly realised that we didn't have the twenty-five cents toll we had to pay at the other end.

"Blast it!" I said. "Have another look through the glove box, will you Muxy. We need twenty-five cents rather urgently."

"There's nothing left in there," he said, "I cleared it out this morning, remember?"

"We'll just have to tell them we'll pay them later."

"I think they only take your name and address," said Muxy. "We can send them the money when we get some again."

"Yeah, we'll give them our last address, that'll keep them happy. Bloody nuisance, though. We don't want to bring too much attention to the condition this car's in at the moment. Blast it! Why does a man have to go broke in a place like this?"

"I'm sure something'll happen," said Muxy. "It always does."

"It had better happen pretty smartly if it's going to get us out of this lot," I remarked.

It happened smarter than I was ready for. As we approached the toll gates two Harbour Bridge uniforms singled us out of the traffic and directed us into the far left-hand lane and made us pull up ten yards short of the toll booth.

"Here's trouble!" I said to Muxy. "Let me do the talking."

And suddenly we were surrounded by people, including at least two uniformed policemen. Then I realised that a man in a suit was trying to shake my hand and my window was stuck halfway up. They were filming us with a TV camera!

"Congratulations!" the bloke was saying, "on being the five-millionth vehicle to cross the bridge since its opening by the Right Honourable So-and-So, on July the something, nineteen something-or-other!"

Then the camera director asked us to drive through so they could get shots of us paying the five-millionth twenty-five cents to the toll collector.

"But we haven't . . ." said Muxy.

"Shut up," said I.

And when they waved us through I pretended to put twenty-five cents into the toll collector's hand.

Photographs flashed and everyone started clapping. But the camera director stopped us and asked if we'd be good enough to go back through and do it again, "and would the toll collector try to look a little more – let's say – happier, this time?" he suggested.

I pretended to take the twenty-five cents back out of the toll collector's still-open hand and reversed through. This time it went off okay. The toll-collector, getting into the swing of it, even pretended to put our imaginery twenty-five cents in his till. then we had to get out of the car and listen to a speech in which another besuited gent told everyone what a great outfit the Harbour Bridge Authority was. Everyone clapped. Then he introduced another gent, who congratulated us once again and informed the assembled crowd what these two fortunate gentlemen had won for themselves: (and he read it out from a sheet of paper) – "A cheque for one hundred and fifty dollars, with the compliments of the Harbour Bridge Authority!" And he handed me an envelope. There was much clapping. (What a great outfit the Harbour Bridge Authority was!) He held up his hand.

"A leather steering-wheel cover and a leather key-holder, valued at eighteen dollars and ninety-nine cents, courtesy of the Tanning Leather Company!"

Applause!

"A set of lambskin car-seat covers, worth eighty-seven dollars-fifty, from Sheepskin Products Limited! – A carton of car-care products, worth thirty-three dollars, from the Car Valet Company! – A car baby-seat, valued at one hundred and thirteen dollars, from Baby-safe Limited! – A free car wash and groom, worth fifteen-sixty, from the Car-Kleen Company! A car radio and speakers, valued at two hundred and forty-nine dollars from PYE!

– A complete free tune-up from the Insta-tune Company! – An oil change, lube and a full tank of gas from the All-nite Service Station. – A book of petrol vouchers, worth two hundred dollars, (more applause) with the compliments of the Atlantic Oil Company! – And a complete set of Firestone Radials, including a spare, valued at five hundred and twenty-six dollars, donated by the Firestone Tyre Company!" More applause.

Then he asked us if we'd like the opportunity to say a few words of thanks to the Harbour Bridge Authority and the sponsors of the prizes. The cameras moved in on us and the M.C. strode forward and shoved the microphone into Muxy's hand. There was silence from the crowd as he began to speak.

"Ladies and Gentlemen," he said. "Thank you very much for all the nice prizes. We weren't expecting them. The oil-change and the tyres and the petrol are exactly what we need at the moment, but if we could have the money instead of the car radio and baby seat and all that other stuff, we'd be very grateful because we need money more than the gear just now . . ."

Caused a bit of consternation in the ranks, that did. The M.C. bloke was pretty good, though. He took over and tried to make a big joke out of it, giving everyone a chance to laugh ourselves out of it. He wound the show up by saying that if we'd be good enough to call this number (and he gave us his card) any time after nine tomorrow morning, he'd personally see that we received our prizes.

As soon as we got away from them we turned around and went back over the bridge into town, to get the Harbour Bridge Authority's cheque cashed.

"Stiffen the rooks!" was all I could think of to say. "What

about that, Muxy?"

"I told you something would happen," he said, looking out the window at the yacht-basin. "It always does."

We booked into a motel that night and watched Muxy on Telly, telling them about our requirements. Then we ate everything they had on the menu in the motel restaurant and went to sleep with the telly on.

Muxy's television appearance was a great success. When we rang our Mr Rutledge next day he said that Muxy's story had captured people's interest, and the television station had given him the names and addresses of people who'd rung in offering to buy our surplus prizes. We found his office, took delivery of our prizes and the list of buyers, thanked him, and spent the rest of the day getting the Dodge attended to and the new tyres fitted.

That night we stayed at another motel, and the next day it took us almost the whole day to find the people and do our deals. They all wanted to keep us drinking tea and talking, and although the radio, the baby-seat, the seat-covers and stuff were worth about five hundred dollars, with Muxy on the job we ended up with three hundred and twenty dollars and the two hundred dollars worth of petrol-vouchers on us when we left town and headed north. The Dodge was running like a bird on its brand new radials, my typewriter was un-pawned – I must have still been a bit bewildered by it all, otherwise I'd never have agreed to let Muxy have a drive of the Dodge when we found a quiet stretch of road. I know, I shouldn't have. I can only think that the madness that surrounded us then must have affected my judgement.

He hadn't done much driving, he reckoned, never had a car of his own or anything, but he was keen to give it a try. He'd driven tractors, a motorbike once, a truck once, the orphanage van round the football field a few times – and he could ride a pushbike real good; nearly got a paper-round once. Sounded promising. I let him have a drive late at night when there was nothing much else on the road.

And he wasn't too bad, either. You had to be careful not to let him get flustered, which wasn't the easiest thing in the world to do. He was unexciting as far as speed went, but that was perfectly okay with me, there was excitement enough when he started to panic in unexpectedly heavy traffic or some other tricky situation. But our luck was holding out and Muxy was so delighted with his driving progress that I found myself catching his enthusiasm. I even found myself getting involved in giving him a few simple instructions; things like keeping to the left on blind corners, and changing down before the vehicle started chugging back and forth on the slack in the transmission.

It was obvious by this time that we were going to have to get our act together. We couldn't go on sleeping in the front of the Dodge. For one thing we weren't getting enough sleep, and for another we were looking too scruffy to attract any good luck that might be around. We were going to have to economise, too. We talked it over and decided to get a tent and a bit of camping gear. A small gas stove, a hatchet, and some other things we didn't already have.

The Dodge was packed tight to the windows by the time we'd stamped all this extra gear in, but it worked pretty good. We stopped at camping grounds, or rest areas along the road and other suitable places. It made us look and feel a bit less like what we were – gentlemen of slender means.

Being able to have a shave and a bath in a basin of hot water inspired us to throw our dirty clothes into a laundry when we found one, and our general standard of living was thereby raised. Muxy's surfcaster on the car lent us a faint air of holidaymakers.

Muxy was hopeless at camping at first. He burnt a hole in our new tent with a candle the second night we used it. He had no idea of how to light a fire, or what to buy or how to cook it. But once he did learn these things he became good at them and did more than his share of it. He liked camping life, he said, because it was easier to keep track of everything when you had to pack it all up next day.

For the next few weeks Muxy's interest was centred on driving the Dodge. He fell in love with it. He even washed it one day and made us late getting away because he didn't want to drive it on the dusty road while it was still wet.

As soon as we'd get up in the morning he'd start electioneering to get to do the driving that day. And once he was behind the wheel he liked to talk, to show how in-control he was. It made him funny to listen to at times because he was inclined to panic easy when something happened in the traffic.

"Y'know, Gav," he said one day as he was barrelling up State Highway One at an unsteady fifty to sixty-five kph in light traffic, "I think I'd like to have a go at taxi-driving."

"No kidding!"

"No, I'm serious. I just know I'm meant to do something in the driving line of work. I've got the right kind of temperament for . . . BLOODY HELL. . . . – DID YOU SEE WHAT THAT DAMN LUNATIC DID JUST THEN, GAV. – what was I saying? Oh yes, some sort of a driving job. Maybe delivering stuff for people, or something like that."

"My oath," I said. "Watch out for this car in front, Muxy, he's turning right."

Before long I could close my eyes and tell what was happening by the way Muxy drove the car. Slowing down, a long curve out to the left, followed by a sudden acceleration – and sure enough, an oncoming car. A violent swerve to the left, accompanied by a sudden deceleration, then a slow pick-up of speed again – we were being overtaken. A jerking deceleration and a sudden stab at the brakes meant that a sharp bend was coming up, then a series of erratic swerves as he milked it round the corner. A slowing down, a bit more accelerator, a dab at the brake, a nudge of accelerator, another touch of the brake, and I knew we were about to free-wheel into a major intersection or road works with our foot on the clutch.

How Muxy got us into and out of some of the traffic manoeuvres we were involved in, I'll never know. Things like changing lanes without warning. Switching his blinker light one way and then turning the other. Completely forgetting about the brake and steering wheel while he was changing gear . . . but as I said, our luck was holding out.

We got a puncture miles from anywhere and found a brand new hydraulic jack, with handle, lying right where we'd stopped. Muxy got off three traffic-offence tickets in two days, using a different weak excuse each time. The first traffic officer pulled him up for doing seventy in a fifty kph area. Muxy told him that he'd never had a ticket before and he was very ashamed, and the traffic officer let him off with a warning.

The second traffic officer stopped us for failing to give way to the right and nearly causing an accident. Muxy said he didn't know they were so strict about it, and the officer gave him a lecture on the right-hand-rule, asked for his driver's licence, (Muxy didn't have it with him), and the officer let him off with another warning.

The third traffic officer caught us a beaut.

"Failing to comply with a compulsory-stop sign, sir."

"But I haven't been driving very long," explained Muxy. "I didn't know."

"Do you have your driver's licence with you, sir?"

"The other traffic cop asked me for it, too," said Muxy.

"I see, and you've sent it to them?"

"That's right," I said quickly.

And, believe it or not, that traffic officer let him off with a warning as well. Pretty tinny of Muxy, really, especially considering the feebleness of his stories and the fact that he'd never had a driver's licence in his life.

Muxy and I were both drawn to the north. There was something about the pleasant uneventfulness of it up there. It was like a breather on a long climb; a patch of hard sand on a walk round the coast, or coming to tarseal after hours of gravel road.

By the time we'd drifted as far as Kaitaia, Muxy had spotted several signs saying that there was a big surf-fishing contest on Ninety-Mile Beach in a couple of days time. He was keen to have a go at it and I was interested to see what it was all about, so we bought some food and bait, filled our water container, and went and camped out at the beach.

Muxy untied his rod off the car for the first time in months. It was bent, but he said it would be all right with a bit of use. Next day he found his bag of fishing gear in the back seat and spent hours making up traces and winding nylon off reels onto other reels and such. I hadn't realised he was so deeply into it. It was hard to imagine Muxy ever having had the opportunity to become experienced at surfcasting.

"Where did you pick it up, Muxy?"

"At the orphanage. They used to take us out to Piha or Muriwai Beach every week during the summer. And I've read every magazine article that's come out about it for years."

He went down the beach and fished for a while that afternoon, but he didn't catch anything. Next morning we were still asleep when the fishing contest tent started going up beside us. We forced our sleeping bags and tent into the Dodge and paid two dollars fifty for Muxy to enter the contest.

He was excited but not letting on. I could tell by the way his voice went expressionless, like the man who reads the weather forecast on the radio.

"Hell, you blokes must have got here early to be first onto the beach," I heard someone say to him. "I got here at six o'clock and I'm about half a mile back down the road!"

“We got here two days ago,” Muxy told him.

“Hell man! You must be keen. Good luck to you, you deserve to win it!”

Muxy was tickled pink about that, he wasn’t often the object of other people’s admiration.

By the time the contest opened, at eight-thirty, the place was packed with people, and vehicles were backed up as far as you could see. I’d had no idea surf-fishing was such a big thing. With us going first in the old red Dodge, a stream of cars and trucks and jeeps and bikes and pedestrians, plus a few horses, poured out onto the Ninety-Mile Beach and raced like a goldrush up the broad highway of hard grey sand that ran between the ranks of crashing surf and the mounded breasty sandhills, to disappear in a haze of spray away round the curve of the coast.

“Pull up right here, Gav,” said Muxy about five miles up the beach.

We parked high up on the beach and the sumptuous assortment of vehicles continued to pour past us while Muxy set up his gear and fixed his baits the way he liked them. Then he went down and fired his sinker well out beyond the breakers with his first cast. I was impressed.

“There’s a bit of a ditch out there, Gav,” he called out. “If there’s any fish around they ought to come through that.”

I waved agreement and went to sit up on a sandhill to watch the goings-on. It was a beautiful day, sunny and windy, with cloud-shadows racing across everything and a fringe of spray blowing off the tops of the breakers as they rolled forward, rank on rank, to topple thunderously into the turmoil at the waters edge. As far as you could see in each direction, people and vehicles of all shapes and sizes milled about, hurried back and forth and parked at all angles across the beach.

Trouser legs and skirts blown against legs, and children and dogs chasing blown hats and balls and seagulls. A pre-war truck trundled along selling watermelons, another came back the other way selling sweetcorn and kumaras. An ice-cream van darted from group to group, its music blown away on the wind before it reached me. And along the waterline was a flimsy pallisade of rods with their keepers in attendance, all hoping for that big nibble at every moment.

No fish could have got past that lot of enthusiasts, but none seemed to be trying. No one within sight caught anything in the first hour and the pace slowed down somewhat. I gathered that we were waiting for the tide to come in a bit further. I was just thinking of getting some firewood together to make a brew of tea, when,

"Got One! – Got One!"

It was Muxy, and he did have one! About a hundred of us saw his rod quivering and bending; heard him shouting advice to himself as he played it in through the surf! By the bend in his rod and the terrific struggle he was having with it I'd have thought he had a good show of winning the fishing competition, but then someone saw it.

"It's a snapper!" they yelled.

"A little one!" yelled someone else.

They were both right. It was a nice young eating-snapper, weighing three and a quarter pounds, according to the scales of a neighbourly fishermaniac. Everyone perked up and started fishing harder, changed their bait and waited for it.

The tide came in and started going out again. No one on our stretch of beach got another bite all day. Nor did anyone else I saw. The odd ute or truck went back down the beach with people holding up small sharks and things, but it was generally agreed that it was the worst year for fish they'd had since the contest had started.

By the time the contest closed at five o'clock everyone had had enough of it, and a steady stream of vehicles and sunburnt people had been leaving the beach all afternoon. There was hardly anyone but us left on the beach when I made Muxy pack it in. He was still enthusiastic after fishing all day for one bite! I didn't mind that the fishing had been poor, it had been a pleasant day. I was beginning to feel the first prickle of sunburn under my shirt.

We stopped at the official tent, one of the last to weigh-in.

Muxy's snapper was just over three pounds, according to the official scales, and it won the contest for the biggest snapper of the day! They handed Muxy a certificate and a cheque for twelve hundred dollars.

I nearly fell over. I mean to say – damn it – I bent to pick the twelve-hundred-dollar cheque up off the sand behind Muxy, who was showing his certificate around.

By seven o'clock that night we were sitting in a restaurant eating oyster cocktails, toheroa soup, steak and salad and onions and tomatoes and cheesecake and coffee. That sea air makes you hungry.

"I still don't believe it," I was saying. "Twelve hundred bucks for a three-pound snapper. I've thrown away millions at that rate!"

"That's what happens with surfcasting," said Muxy contentedly. "Do you feel like another order of that cheesecake?"

"Sure, why not."

FOUR

Agreement To Purchase

After Kaitaia, we drove up to Cape Reinga because neither of us had ever been right up to the tip of the country before. We walked down past the lighthouse and stood looking where the Pacific Ocean and the Tasman Sea meet in a magnificent rip of choppy, broken water. Hell to try and sail a small boat through, I would have thought, but while we watched a yacht appeared round the point and sailed right into it. When they'd made it safely across the worst of it we got back in the Dodge and headed south again.

We went down the east coast this time, living on mussels, fish, kumaras, wild pork, crayfish and a hen pheasant that a young Maori bloke we'd helped, swore flew into his windscreen. (We saw him again later, riding his horse).

"Broke its blimmin' neck!" he assured us.

Looked more like a .22 bullet had done it, if you asked me.

As we drove away from there, me at the wheel for a change, I couldn't help marvelling at how everything had been falling into place for us lately.

"By strike, Muxy. There's no doubt about you mate!"

"How come?" He was reading a Scrooge McDuck comic.

"Well, when you're down, you're dangerous, and when you're up, you can't throw tails. We should have taken you to the bloody races while you're hot. We could make a fortune with you!"

"I'm just the same as anyone else," he protested.

"You're more than anyone else I've ever met," I said.

"I can't help that. It doesn't worry me, anyway."

"But you take such a hell of a lot of punishment when you're having a bad trot," I said. "Doesn't that put you off a bit?"

"Nar, Gav," he said, "I keep telling you, it all depends on how you look at it. You think I have bad luck, but I don't look at it that way."

"Then I don't suppose you think being the five-millionth car across the Harbour Bridge when we were flat broke and getting all that money and stuff, and winning that fishing contest with that little snapper, and getting off those traffic tickets – and all the other stuff that's been happening to us lately – I suppose you don't think all that was good luck then?"

"That's right. It makes no difference what luck you call things that happen, they happen just the same, and you have to accept them just the same."

"Whether you like it or not, you reckon?"

"Sure, liking or not-liking something can't make it happen or stop it from happening."

"No," I said, "I don't suppose it can, when you put it that way. I just hope this good bit hangs on for a while yet, that's all."

It did. We continued having good luck around the North and

didn't do a tap of work for three months, not even my usual weekly couple of articles for the papers. Didn't seem to have the time, yet we wasted enough of it. We stayed in some places for a week or more, and met some extraordinary people, but then I suppose they must have thought we were a bit unusual ourselves. It was no use trying to explain how we got there, what we were doing there, or where we were going and why.

We were driving up Bayleys Beach one day to see if we could get the car out onto a road at the other end, and away up ahead on a remote stretch of the beach we saw a strange shape that turned out to be an old Maori bloke with a draught horse pulling a single-furrow plough. We stopped for a yarn with him. He lived just beyond the sand dunes there and he was ploughing this patch of beach. He was also accidentally turning up quite a few toheroa, which his wife and two of their grandchildren were gathering in flax kits 'for the pigs'. No sense in wasting all that good tucker, eh!

We accepted a feed of toheroa from the old bloke and camped a bit further up the beach that night and ate them before we left there. There was a thousand-dollar fine for being in possession of toheroa out of season and I wasn't prepared to push our luck that far. Muxy surfcasted a kahawhai that day, using toheroa for bait.

Our luck was still holding the next morning. A four-wheel-drive came along the beach and headed straight for where we were parked.

"Bury those toheroa shells, Muxy," I said. "You never know who this might turn out to be."

It turned out to be two rangers, patrolling the beach. They

pulled up beside the car and got out and asked us what we were doing there. Muxy's surfcasting gear covered that. Then they told us that there was no camping on the beach and we told them we didn't know. One of them was standing right on top of our hastily-covered toheroa shells. It must have made him feel suspicious. They asked if we had any objection to them having a look through the car. We said okay, if they wanted to. They opened the boot and the back door and had a look at the conglomeration of stuff in there and decided not to bother. They told us to be sure and move to a camping ground that night and drove off along the beach.

"I hope they don't run across our old Maori mate," I said. "They'll deal to him if they catch him ploughing up those shellfish."

We couldn't get off the beach at the far end and had to go back past where the old bloke had ploughed up the beach. The tides had washed out all traces of him.

Another day not long after that we were parked at a beach in the far north and Muxy was a bit hacked off with me because I'd thrown his bait away. It had been starting to stink. Now he had nothing to fish with and he liked the look of the far end of the beach for a surfcast. We'd only been there for a few minutes when a couple drove along the beach and pulled up for a yarn. They'd had the net out and had a bucket full of herrings. They gave Muxy half a dozen of them and he was almost rude in his hurry to get up the beach and start fishing. He was out of the car and sorting out his gear almost before we'd stopped.

"I'm putting a wire trace on this time, Gav," he said. "We'll get sharks here."

"How do you know that?" I asked him.

"I'm going to bait-up with herring-heads. You always catch sharks on herring-heads."

"Come on, Muxy. You can't tell that."

"It's true," he said. "Ask anyone."

"What's the difference between a herring's head and any other fish's head?"

"Herring-heads have got a special oil in them that attracts sharks," he explained. "Everyone knows that."

You could only shrug in reply to some of the things Muxy said.

He was ready. He performed his ritual. He carried the baited rod down to the edge of the water as though he was going to throw it in for a sacrifice, then he stepped back two or three steps and then did a little skip forward, at the same time flinging the tip of his rod at the horizon. He let go the line at the exact right moment and the sinker and hooks flew out beyond the waves. He impressed me when he did that. Something Muxy was good at.

He paid out line and brought his rod up the beach a few yards and drove the holder into the sand and set the tension.

"Keep an eye on it, Gav," he said. "When sharks hit you they take a lot of turning around sometimes. If one strikes, grab the rod quick and wind on the drag to slow it down. I'm just going up to the car for the rest of the gear and the bait."

"What if there's no sharks around just here?" I said.

"The herring-heads'll bring them," he said with child-like confidence. "Just keep an eye on the rod until I get back. I won't be a minute."

"Sure, Muxy. No hurry."

He must have just reached the car when it happened. I wasn't watching his rod, I was looking around, when the reel started screaming and the tip of the rod was bent right over and trembling with tension. I ran over and grabbed it out of the holder. There was something big on the end of it. Felt like a train to me. I found the drag and wound it on, but the thing kept stripping off line.

"Muxy!" I yelled. It was the first time I'd ever needed him.

He'd been rummaging and hadn't seen what was going on.

"Hold him, Gav!" he yelled. "Hold him!"

I kept trying to hold him until Muxy got there and pulled the rod off me and began pumping and winding and adding to the drag.

"We've got to turn him round," he yelled. "He's taken nearly all the line!"

He managed to stop the train and turn it round and played it up and down along the beach beyond the waves. Whatever it was, was big all right. Muxy was getting tired but he wouldn't let me give him a spell.

"Good big hunk of a shark this, Gav," he said.

"Are you sure it's not a whale?" I said.

"It's a shark all right," he said. "You always catch sharks on herring-heads. There's a special oil in them that attracts sharks, you know."

"Sure, Muxy."

I saw what it was before Muxy did. I caught a glimpse of it in a wave. It was a shark. About six feet long, bigger than Muxy.

"It's a shark," I said. "I just saw it."

"Of course it's a shark," he said. "What did you think it was?"

It took him the best part of half an hour to play that shark into the shallows, where I got a loop of rope round its tail and we dragged it up onto the beach and bled it.

"It's a grey nurse," said Muxy, looking into its mouth, "and it's swallowed both hooks. We're going to have to cut it open to get them out."

He couldn't wait to get his line baited-up and back in the water, and I was still dragging the first shark towards the car when Muxy shouted. He'd hooked another one. It didn't seem to be as big as the first one, and after about five minutes it got off the hook. Privately I wasn't sorry, we already had more shark than we knew what to do with.

This left Muxy with his last two herring-heads, enough for one more bait-up, and after a while he caught another shark, a small one, about three feet long, and although we hung around there for two more hours, fishing with herring bodies, he didn't get another bite.

We packed it in and cut up our sharks and sold the fillets to a fish shop in Kaitaia for forty dollars, for their fish and chips.

"You can't beat herring-heads for catching sharks," Muxy informed me as we drove north again. "There's a special oil in them that attracts . . ."

"Sure, Muxy. You already mentioned that."

Sometimes when the weather or the tides weren't right and there was nothing to do, we lay around in the tent, reading books and listening to the radio.

I was still pretty chary of flopping into the booze again, and alcohol only made Muxy either silly or sick, so we didn't spend much of our time or money in the pubs. We'd go in and raffle off a couple of crays or a bag of mussels we'd been given, drink a few lemonades and take off.

We did get into a bit of buying and selling when we ran across something interesting now and then. Muxy was actually getting better at recognising the value of things and he made an especially good deal over an outboard motor a bloke wanted to quit in a hurry. Only I still had to be quick to get the money off him whenever he sold something.

Although Muxy was undoubtedly improving, I didn't feel that he was ready to be trusted with our money yet. We kept our main roll hidden in the boot of the Dodge under the spare wheel, and carried no more than a hundred dollars around with us. And our luck was so good that at one stage we didn't have to dip into the boot for a month.

Then our luck changed again. This disquieting fact only dawned on me when I realised that Muxy had a broken finger in a splint, a sprained other wrist, a cut on his foot from broken glass, and a big yellow bruise on his eyebrow – all from things that had happened to him over the past two days.

And what's more, we hadn't had a financial windfall in over a week. I discreetly took over the driving.

"How much of our travelling cash have we got left, Muxy?" I asked him.

"Not that much," he said, a little too quickly.

"How much?"

"Two dollars, maybe three with the change in the glovebox," he admitted.

"Thought so," I said grimly. "It's happened."

"What's happened?"

"Our luck's changed again, that's what. I don't know what you call it, but I reckon it'll be all up-hill going for another stretch now."

"Depends how you look at it," he shrugged.

“Sure does,” I had to agree.

Another ominous sign was the wasps. We were camped in a place we'd used a couple of times before at a beach with no name. There were heaps of wasps around the north that year and there was a nest of them in a bank near our camp. They hung around our food a fair bit, but if you don't bother with wasps they won't bother with you. That's what Muxy reckoned anyway. But he changed his tune next morning when he got up to light our fire and a wasp stung him through a hole he'd torn in the seat of his pants the day before.

“Ow! – We've got to do something about these blasted wasps, Gav,” he called out, slapping at himself. “They're getting too cheeky altogether!”

“Uh-huh,” I grunted from inside my sleeping bag in the tent.

“I'll fix them for good and all,” I heard him say.

I must have dozed off for a few moments and the next thing I heard was Muxy calling out, “Gav! Come and give us a hand. I've got these wasps beat!”

I wriggled my way to the doorway of the tent and there was Muxy, holding a cardboard box over the entrance of the wasps' nest. Wasps were humming and buzzing inside the box. I could hear them from where I was.

“I've got 'em bottled up in here,” he said. “Just grab something to hold this box here and they're trapped!”

But he hadn't made allowances for the wasps that were outside the nest when he put the box over it. They were gathering in an angry little swarm around him. A handful of them hovered around me. I slapped at them and they went into top gear. I pulled the bag up around my ears.

"Hurry up, Gav," said Muxy. "There's a few I've missed!"

"I'm not getting out of this sleeping bag," I told him. "I've got no strides on. And don't forget that wasps don't just sting you once," I added. "They can go up your leg like a sewing machine."

"What am I going to do," he said. "I can't let this box go now."

He was right about that. If he let go the box it was going to fall off the bank and release several thousand wasps that were definitely being bothered with. And he had only seconds before the ones outside started on him.

The tide was in and it was about forty yards to the water.

"You're going to have to make a run for the sea and dive in," I said.

By this time there were dozens of hacked-off wasps hovering around him, and he only had one spare hand to try and fight them off with.

"Oh hell!" he said, and he let go the box and sprinted across the beach, with a frightening stream of wasps after him. I could hear them as they passed. I never knew Muxy could run that fast. Then a bunch of wasps came at me and I had to take cover in my sleeping bag.

I couldn't tell how Muxy had got on. They could have stung him to death for all I knew, and I couldn't find out because every time I stuck my head out of the bag the wasps attacked me. They must have been watching.

After a very long couple of hours the wasps seemed to have settled down. I dragged my pants into the bag and put them on, with great difficulty. Then I cautiously got out of the bag and began to move towards the beach to find out what had happened to Muxy. They let me get ten yards away from my sleeping bag before they sent in a squadron. I got stung three times before I could get back in the bag. I would have given plenty for a can of flyspray that day.

After a while I had an idea. I wriggled my way out to the beach inside the bag, and when wasps came at me I only had to pull my head in and wait for them to withdraw and regroup. I got to the top of the beach in time to see Muxy running back into the water waving his arms. They'd let him get halfway up the beach before attacking him again.

This was getting serious. The wasps I'd met before would have given up long before this. Goodness knows how many times Muxy had been stung already. I wriggled back to the camp, encountering a few stray platoons of patrolling wasps on the way, and got Muxy's sleeping bag and wriggled back to the beach with it.

The tide was halfway out by this time and I was wet by the time I'd wriggled out to within earshot of Muxy, who was sitting out in the breakers. During what appeared to be a lull in enemy operations he made a dash for his sleeping bag, but being wet he had a bit of trouble getting into it and was stung twice more by prowling wasps before he was safely inside it. He'd been stung about twenty times around his face and neck and arms, including a couple more through the hole in his pants.

"They could kill a man, Gav!" he called out from inside his bag.

"You're lucky they haven't!" I called back.

"What are we going to do?"

"We'll have to wait till dark and then get the hell out of here," I said. "They usually knock off at night."

We wriggled back to the camp and sneaked some bread and cheese into our bags and ate. Then we slept on and off in our wet sleeping bags. It turned into a stinking hot day but it was still unsafe to get out of our bags. We kept trying but it was just no good. We had to sweat it out.

"What was that you said about having these wasps trapped, Muxy?"

When it was properly dark we cautiously got out of our bags and stood there, checking it out. It was okay, the wasps had all gone to bed for the night. We pulled down the tent and loaded up the car and retreated from the scene of battle.

"You never want to muck around with those wasps' nests, Gav," said Muxy seriously. "They could sting a man to death, you know."

The bloody audacity of him!

It had been a long day and we were in for a longer night, driving around looking for somewhere to camp. You never seem to be able to find a place when you need one badly, but the worst part of it as far as I was concerned was the apprehension I always felt with the growing certainty that we were in for another 'touch of the Muxies'.

Muxy had been trying to get the window on his side to stay up, and just then it fell down into the door. We heard the glass shatter inside the door when he slammed it a couple of times later. This seemed like an omen to me. Maybe I was being unfair to Muxy, but after all I'd been through with the man I didn't blame myself for being apprehensive.

We had just over a hundred dollars left under the spare wheel in the boot, which if we were lucky, should have cushioned us against the first onset of ill-fortune that I felt sure was overtaking us. But we weren't being lucky. I was still trying to figure out our safest course when we arrived back in Auckland through not being able to think of anywhere else to go.

And so, almost exactly a year after we'd first teamed-up together, Muxy and I were back where we started. It had been an interesting year, no denying that, but I'd had enough holidaying and living off our luck to go on with. Travelling around and living out of the Dodge was beginning to pall on Muxy, too, so we rented a two-bedroom flat in Herne Bay (cream and brown and poky – the usual thing) and unloaded some of the gear out of the poor old Dodge into it, and found things we hadn't seen since we'd shifted out of our last flat.

We didn't have enough money left for the next lot of rent, and no prospects of getting any more. The bottom of the barrel was looming up again, and we could hardly expect to be the six-millionth car across the harbour bridge.

Then I rang my ex-wife to find out how they were doing, and learnt that our house had been sold, and after her lawyer had finished with the $22,000.00 left over after mortgage repayments, I had a cheque for three thousand dollars to pick up. My ex was as hacked-off as I was about the whole hassle. We had a good chat, came to an amicable arrangement about maintenance, and arranged to arrange a bit of time together when me and my 'boyfriend' were settled in.

I rang up her lawyer and went round to collect my portion of the pickings. He had the decency to try and show me where all the money had gone.

"And we haven't been able to contact you, you realise, Mr Midwinter. In your absence we had no alternative but to go ahead with our claims . . ."

"That's okay mate," I said. "No hard feelings. I'm just pleased to have the whole thing wound up. Would you make the cheque out for cash please."

He did that. Three thousand and two dollars and fifty-one cents.

I cashed the cheque on the way home and put it with the remains of our stash under my mattress. I had the idea of doing something with it.

"I've been thinking," I said to Muxy.

"What about?"

"This money we've got. I reckon we ought to invest some of it in something. We'll never hang onto it the way we're going."

"Invest it in what?"

"Well land would have to be the best. It has to increase in value."

"I've always wanted to own a bit of land," he said eagerly. "We could have it put in both our names," he suggested. (Muxy was always keen to get tied up with you in legal matters because of him being an orphan).

"Sure," I said. "I don't know what kind of land we're going to get for three thousand bucks, though. It might just be enough for a deposit on a section somewhere."

"I'm on for that!" said Muxy.

"Okay then, we'll keep our eyes open for a likely deal eh? With our kind of luck we could just end up with something."

"Good idea, you're on!" said Muxy.

After a week of hanging around the flat doing little more than eat, we decided to make a move. I was fairly sure I could talk a couple of editors into taking articles off me if I could convince them I was off the grog for good this time, so next morning I went into the city to look them in the eye about it. Muxy was going to try for a job at the zoo and then come back and clean up the flat. He was there when I got home that afternoon.

"Guess what!" I said.

"You got accepted!" he said. "But guess what?"

"You got the job at the zoo!"

“Nope, better than that!”

“I give up, what?” I said suspiciously.

“I’ve found our land investment!” he announced.

“Cut it out, Muxy. We only got the idea yesterday.”

“That’s what I mean,” he said, earnestly grasping my sleeve. “It must have been meant to happen!”

“Explain,” I said, shaking my sleeve loose. “This is all a bit too instantaneous for my liking.”

“Well, I was on my way over to the zoo this morning and I saw this land agent’s place, so I just went in and told the bloke how we had three thousand dollars and wanted to invest some of it in some kind of land or maybe a section somewhere – just how we decided . . .”

“And he told you he had the very thing,” I interrupted.

“That’s right! It just came on the market this morning. Hasn’t even been advertised. Half an acre – and this’ll rock you – it’s right here in Herne Bay!”

I ran in and lifted the corner of my mattress and let it drop on what was left of our money and went slowly back to the kitchen, gathering control.

“Where’s the rest of our money, Muxy?” I asked politely.

“I had to pay twelve hundred dollars deposit. We’ve got two years to pay the rest off.”

"The rest?" I enquired.

"Yes, the full price is seven thousand, nine hundred and ninety-five dollars. The bloke said it was a real bargain. He wants us to offer him first refusal when we sell it, as a favour for him letting us have it so cheap."

"Let me get this straight," I said. "You paid a land agent twelve hundred bucks deposit on half an acre of ground in Herne Bay here?"

"That's right!"

"Did you sign anything?"

"Only an Agreement-to-Purchase thing. We're supposed to go back within seven days and sign the transfer of title and the rest of it. I've told them we want it put in both our names."

"I see," I said calmly. "And did you go and have a look at this half acre of ground?"

"No, I haven't long been back from taking the money up to them. Besides, I wanted us both to see it together for the first time. It's my first land I've ever owned, you know."

"Where is it?"

He gave me a piece of paper he'd been holding.

"Here's the address. They showed me where it is on the map. It's out near the harbour."

"Fifty-four Gundry Road," I read out. "I suppose the next thing to do is go and have a look at it."

We got into the Dodge and found Gundry Road without too much trouble, right out at the edge of Herne Bay. A short, steep little road, it was, with a turning-circle at the bottom. And just beyond the turning-circle the ground dropped away into a gully so sharply that they'd had to put up a safety fence.

Yes it was a real steep little gully, that one. And we'd just put a twelve-hundred dollar deposit on it and signed an agreement to purchase it. We didn't even get out of the car.

"Do you think that could be it?" asked Muxy uneasily.

"That'll be it all right," I said. "That last house there is number fifty-two."

"It's a helluva steep down there," he said, leaning out the window.

"Yep."

"What do you reckon, Gav?"

"I reckon we've been ripped off," I said. "That's what I reckon, YOU BLOODY IDIOT!"

"But I didn't know it was going to be steep like that," he protested. "They didn't say anything about it being steep."

I started the Dodge and drove back up Gundry Road.

"We could go back and tell them we've changed our minds and

get our money back," he suggested.

"After you signing that Agreement-to-Purchase – they'd just laugh at you. We're bloody well stuck with it, that's what."

"Couldn't we fill it up or something?"

"What the hell do you think we're going to fill it up with?" I said angrily. "Bloody newspaper?"

"Let's open a rubbish-tip," he said. "I like tips!"

"I've had just about enough of your bloody ideas for one day," I told him shortly. "What the hell did you want to go and give our money – my money – to some sharp land agent for? You could have waited and checked with me about it," I added, pulling up at the flat.

"But I felt right about it, Gav. And I wanted to give you a surprise."

"Well I don't feel right about it, and I'm not very pleasantly surprised, either. I don't know why I bother with you, Muxy, I really don't. You're nothing but a bloody hassle most of the time!"

Muxy got out of the car without saying anything else, and I drove into town and went to a movie for somewhere to think. I picked up some Kentucky fries and bean salad for us on the way home, but when I got there Muxy was gone. And although he'd left a lot of his gear behind he'd taken his surfcaster from the corner beside the wardrobe. He'd taken some of our money as well, which was fair enough. He'd have gone through more of it than that if he'd stayed.

I didn't know what to feel about Muxy taking off at first. Maybe I shouldn't have been so heavy on him, but it was how I felt at the time. I was really fond of him, like a brother, but he was a hell of a worry at times. It was some relief to think I wouldn't have to keep aware of what he was doing all the time.

With Muxy gone I got a bit of writing done on the third day. A bit less the day after that, none the day after that, some the day after that, and quite a lot the day after that. In other words, it was about the same as when he was there.

During the next few weeks I made a few friends around the district, most of whom enquired about what had happened to my friend. I told them we'd decided to part because of starting to get on each other's nerves and that was usually enough to shut them up about it.

I cleaned out the Dodge and saw the floor in the back seat for the first time in memory. Enough money was coming in to pay the rent and buy food. It was a bit dull, if anything, I'd decided but it was peaceful. I saw my ex-wife and daughter twice. They were doing okay and none of us got around to suggesting a next time. Nothing left there.

Living alone again was good for me in a way. I realised I'd been using Muxy. It was noticeably harder for me to keep away from the pubs, without him there for me to concentrate on. I had to get used to using other things. At one stage I was standing around in pubs yarning with the blokes and drinking Coke, but I knew what I was doing. It was curiosity mainly, and I must confess to a feeling of power as I walked out the door knowing that the old booze didn't have me helpless any more. Only scared.

I came home with a load of laundry one afternoon and I'd just put it down when the tip of Muxy's surfcaster come through the door, followed by a bursting army kit-bag and Muxy's ridiculous grin.

"What brings you back?" was all I could think of to say.

"Didn't feel right, Gav," he said, dumping his bag on the sofa.

"Didn't feel right to me, either," I agreed, taking the surfcaster off him before he did some damage with it. "Have you had a feed?"

I'd realised that it was easier on me to worry about what Muxy was doing when he was around, than to imagine what he might be up to somewhere else. Maybe he'd be a bit less harebrained, now that he'd had time to think about it . . .

"I still think we ought to open a tip, Gav," he said when he'd finished eating everything in the flat.

"You don't say."

"Yep, I feel right about it."

"I'm not comitting myself," I said cautiously. "We'd have to go right into every aspect of it before you'd get me interested in anything like that."

"What would we have to do first?"

"See a lawyer and find out what's involved, I suppose," I said. "But don't do anything final without checking with me, okay?"

"Okay," he agreed, "I'll find a lawyer tomorrow."

"We'll have to go up to that land agency tomorrow morning, and sign those papers. Your mate's been threatening to enforce that Agreement-to-Purchase you signed. There's a wad of letters from them among that stuff on the sideboard there, if you're interested."

He grabbed the letters and began shuffling through them. "I don't know, Gav, but I just feel right about this tip idea. I like tips."

"Well don't go getting your hopes too high," I warned him. "The whole thing looks like a dead loss to me. I don't for a moment believe they'd ever let anyone open a rubbish tip there. No, there's not much chance of it coming to anything."

FIVE

Midwinter & Muxworthy Ltd

The lawyer Muxy had gone to was as skeptical of the whole tip scheme as I was, but the letter he got back from the Auckland Regional Authority put a different slant on the whole thing. They regarded the property in question as a potentially dangerous area and agreed that it should be filled in. They would give favourable consideration to an application to open it as a refuse tip – for inorganic household refuse only – provided there was provision made for them to supervise, inspect and close down or take over the operation at their pleasure. There was a long list of the things we must, should, could and couldn't do. They were very strict about fires, for instance. They were prohibited. And the regulations they brought to our attention were overwhelming.

However Muxy 'felt right' about it and waded through one hassle after another, dragging me into it whenever he got intimidated by the bureaucrats, and finally it came to the point where his lawyer advised us to form a company. Which we duly did, not without some unspoken trepidation on my part. Midwinter-Muxworthy Limited, we agreed to call ourselves, though I made Muxy agree to use M-M Ltd. (No point in exposing ourselves to unnecessary ridicule).

Muxy was getting more excited every day. All we had to do now was buy a tractor of some sort for pushing all this alleged garbage we were going to handle, over the edge.

We picked an old diesel Fordson with a blade on the back, a loader on the front, rubber tyres with some meat left on them, and it seemed to start easy. Seven hundred and fifty bucks; we were nearly broke again. I knew that if this tip thing didn't work we were going to be in worse shape than ever, but what the hell! Some of Muxy's attitudes seemed to be a bit contagious. I wished he'd catch some of my meanness, to balance his distressing tendency to give our money away.

Our first job with the tractor was to lift the safety fence away in sections from the front of our rubbish tip. (We stacked them to one side and sold them later to one of our customers for five dollars).

Then we wrote,

INORGANIC (ONLY) REFUSE $3.00 A LOAD – ANY SIZE on a piece of board and nailed it onto the post underneath the GUNDRY ROAD sign, and although it could only be seen from one direction, we never added to it. It was the only advertising we ever did there.

We took twelve dollars that first afternoon, and the next day, Sunday, we took thirty dollars. In our first week of business we made nearly as much as we spent, and we already had enough stuff stacked around the bit of flat ground between the road and the tip-head to have me worried.

"Look here, Muxy, what's all this corrugated iron doing here?"

"We're not putting that over the tip," he said indignantly. "It's good iron, that!"

"What else are we going to do with it? We can't leave it there. And what about all these old mattresses and carpet and stuff under all this polythene here?"

"We'll sell it."

"Who the hell to?"

"People who come to dump rubbish. They can take a load of this good stuff away with them."

"I doubt it," I said. "They're not going to want to swap one load of junk for another."

"This isn't junk," he protested. "Someone could have a use for all this stuff here. You wait, I bet when people get to know it's here they'll come and get it all right. We might even be able to charge them a few cents for some of those good tools and things!"

"Now look here, Muxy. We're in business now, and we're going to have overheads, costs and all sorts of other expenses. You've got to stop letting people off their tip fees, and we must charge people for everything they want to take away from here. It's the only way we've got any chance of making this thing work."

"I realise that, Gav, but I'd rather give something away than risk ripping them off by charging too much."

"If anyone wants to buy anything, let me deal with them," I said.

"No," he said. "I'd like to do that part. I'll charge them."

"Well come over here and we'll work out what we ought to get for some of it. This window frame here, now that's got to be worth at least five bucks to anyone that needs one . . ."

"I went on trying to give him an idea of what I reckoned his junk was worth, but he went all vague and I knew I wasn't getting through to him any more.

"Not that I think we're going to sell any more than the odd thing. Most of it's going to have to go over the tip in the finish anyway," I said.

I was wrong again. It was slow at first but as more people got to find out about us we became busier and busier. Within two months we were making more out of what we sold than out of the tip fees. We had to buy a portable garage and set it up at the tip so we could keep all our valuable merchandise under lock and key at night. Muxy was still keeping too much stuff from going over the edge and it became something of a game between us; while he was under-charging someone for something inside the 'shop', I'd hop onto the tractor and start bucketing some of the doubtful stuff over the tip. When Muxy came out shouting for me to stop, I'd pretend I hadn't realised he was saying it.

It wasn't easy to guess what was saleable and what wasn't, and we had to find out by experience. We were getting books and bricks and hardboard and timber and doors, furniture of all kinds, cushions, bedding, curtains, cutlery, cloth, cradles, towels, radios, boots, crockery, clothing, paint, toys, musical instruments, wallpaper, toasters, heaters, irons, sacks, boxes, crates, cartons, trunks, suitcases, tins, drums, bags, lawnmowers, sewing machines, electric and petrol motors, ropes, hoses, pushchairs, wire, scrap-metal, basins, bowls, bolts and bottles, to make mention of but a small selection of it, and we found that much of the stuff people were dumping was of better quality than what they were replacing it with.

They started coming from miles away because it was cheap and you could always get in. Gundry Road had never been so busy; if they didn't come to conveniently get rid of their rubbish, they came to get in on some of the ridiculous bargains Muxy was handing out.

We had to open a bank account because we had to do something with the cardboard box full of money under my bed. We made it a joint account, so that both of us had to sign the cheque when we wanted to pay for anything or draw money out, to save arguments.

Muxy was taking driving lessons and the driving-school bloke confided to me one night that if Muxy failed the written test he was taking next day (his fifth), the driving-school was going to acknowledge its first failure.

But Muxy passed the test and got his driver's licence, which at first he flashed around as though it was an Olympic Gold Medal.

They kept coming to the Gundry Road Tip; ladies with children in the back seat and rubbish in the boot, retired gents with immaculate cars and small trailer-loads of thoroughly worn-out junk; shopkeepers short of space, with truckloads of cardboard packaging material and blown fluorescent tubes; Saturday shed-cleaner-outers, usually always good for at least one fixable lawnmower; people shifting and getting rid of stuff not worth paying for the transport of; and quite a few from Herne Bay who'd discovered they suddenly had a tip handy and decided to have a clean-out. Trucks, vans, cars, trailers, station wagons, motorbikes and pedestrians. And Muxy soon had his regular do-it-yourselfers sorting through his conglomeration for handy bargains.

We had a bit of trouble with people trying to dump organic

stuff on us, but only at first. Once they got sent away with it again they got the message. We had to be strict about that.

It got that way that we were working till dark most nights, getting the day's mess sorted out, and we did quite a bit of business with people in the evenings after work.

Then one day two men from the A.R.A. came and told us to stop selling stuff from our tip premises immediately, otherwise they'd close us down altogether. So we rented a big old shop in Ponsonby Road and bought a five-hundred dollar Bedford van to cart our merchandise up there in. After that we used the garage at the tip site for an office and to store stuff in for the shop.

Muxy took over the shop. He had a big M-M Ltd painted on the window and sold out his first shop full of our best stuff for eighty-two dollars. He was still improving, but only very slowly.

"Y'know Gav," he had the cheek to say to me one day, "it's actually better to give someone a good deal than to give them something outright. Makes 'em feel like they actually own the thing. And they always seem to come back again."

"No wonder they come back, the way you give stuff away," I told him. "You're a mug, you know, Muxy. They already know you're the easiest rip-off around here. You rip yourself off!"

"I'm charging a hell of a lot more than I used to," he said.

"You could easily afford to double your prices. You'd still be practically giving the stuff away."

"I don't think I could do that," he said, slightly shocked.

"Well keep trying," I said. "I'd better get back to the tip. I'll bring another load of stuff if it gets quiet down there later on, otherwise I'll bring it when I knock off."

It could only have been a week or so after we'd opened the shop when I first heard it referred to as the Double-M, and that became its name. The Double-M, and Muxy became an institution in Ponsonby Road. He treated his customers as though they were doing him a favour, not because it was a good attitude for a shopkeeper to have, but because he believed it. They came in a steady stream, many of them bringing friends to show them this strange shop with the strange man who sold strange stuff at strange prices. I used to get a kick out of watching him with them, but he didn't like me hanging around his shop. There were other second-hand shops in Ponsonby Road, but nothing like Muxy's one.

Things were easier, but busier, with me running the tip on my own. I could sort out what I thought should go up to the shop without having to argue with Muxy about it. If he'd seen some of the things I shoved over into the tip, he'd have fainted. Anything obviously good, or that was inexplicably selling like hot cakes lately, I loaded into the van and took it up to the shop and put it where Muxy ordered, when I got a quiet spell.

As we became better known we were approached by antique dealers, car restorers, house renovators, architects, builders, farmers, ordinary people, all assuming we knew what we were doing, and wanting us to keep a lookout for something or other they were interested in.

Then we started doing business with demolition firms, and car wreckers, excavation contractors, factories, the A.R.A. itself. And some of the contracts we got were worth hundreds of dollars.

Within four months we'd paid off what we owed on our 'land' and still had money in the bank.

Muxy had taken over the banking because he was learning a business system from a Chinese greengrocer and another from a lady newsagent. It seemed to be working okay. I just gave him the bag of money from the tip and he'd count it out to the nearest three dollars and tell me how many customers I'd had that day. He kept a book on it so I didn't need to. If I needed cash I simply transferred it from the tip fee bag into my hip pocket and we had that many less customers that week. Muxy paid himself sixty-five dollars a week and wrote it up in a special wages book. He tried to get me into doing it that way, but I didn't see the need to alter the way we had it already.

Not that either of us had much time to spend money these days. We were very busy, and on our days off Muxy worked on his account books and I slept and watched television on a colour set we rented. Our only extravagance was eating out at various restaurants around town two or three times a week after work.

It got too busy at the tip for me to keep up with. I had an honesty box on an Alfa Laval cream-separator stand, but it really needed somebody to be there to organise where each load was dumped, and I was always having to drop everything and run a load of stock up to the Double-M to keep Muxy going.

There'd been this bloke hanging around quite a bit. He was furnishing a house and was after a decent lounge suite. He'd taken two of them home and exchanged them when better ones came in. One day when he'd been helping me carry a kerosene fridge into the garage, I asked him if he wanted a part-time job. He did.

His name was Daniel Kupa. He was a Cook Islander, who'd been in this country for two and a half years, and he was a carpenter by trade. He'd lost his job when the company he was working for folded, and he wouldn't go on the dole, even though he was having a bit of trouble keeping up the payments on the house he was buying in McKelvie Street. His wife and kids were still in Rarotonga, waiting for him to get his act together and send for them.

Daniel was in his early forties, I guessed, a bit heavy-built, with a great big smile and a wide gap between his front teeth. He was so energetic; so cheerful and cheeky and honest and untidy that Muxy and I both wanted him to come and work for us full time. He kept us hanging between yes and no for a day before taking us up on it.

Daniel was so good at running the tip that after the first month I had to think away a feeling of intruding whenever I went into his office. He didn't like me driving his tractor, either, and always had some feeble reason why he didn't want that particular heap of absolute rubbish pushed over the edge just yet. And I was hardly ever quick enough to beat him to a customer, no matter how busy we were. He very soon picked up what to keep and what to throw away, except for clothing, his standards were way down in that department. People were always throwing away better clothes than he was wearing, but they hardly noticed that because of his laughter and teasing of them. Daniel and the customers enjoyed each other. He was good value.

I ended up with the only other job that was going – carting stuff from the tip to the shop and putting it where Muxy ordered it put.

Guy Fawkes night came round and our tip caught fire. We had

the biggest bonfire in Auckland. It lit up the whole area. Someone in Gundry Road must have got worried and called the Fire Department, because a machine came and parked at the top of the road until it started to die down a bit. Daniel was there when Muxy and I arrived, grinning like a happy devil in the firelight.

As soon as I saw him there I remembered a conversation we'd had that very afternoon about how much more tipping we'd have had if we were only allowed to burn it.

"Bad luck eh boss," he said, grinning from ear to ear at the fire-officer who was standing with us.

"Any idea how it started?" asked the fire-officer.

"Must have been them kids I saw around here before," said Daniel.

A couple of days later we got a snotty letter from the A.R.A. who were not pleased. They warned us if it happened again they'd seriously review our permit. I showed their letter to Daniel.

"If I see them kids around here again, I'll kick their backsides, boss," he assured me.

"We can't afford to have it catch on fire by accident, after this," I said, spearing the A.R.A.'s letter onto the brow tine of a stag's head we filed such things on.

He stopped smiling, "Yeah," he said. "I see what you mean."

Next day Daniel laughed the lady in the house next to us into letting him tap into her water-supply, and he ran a hose down to the dump with a turn-on nozzle. This was something of a miracle because that lady had made several official complaints about our operation.

One morning when Muxy and I were down at the tip loading a treadle-organ into the van, Daniel arrived and told us he needed a fifty-dollar-a-week raise.

"No way," I said, "you're getting above the award already."

"You're welcome to it," said Muxy, "if you need it."

"I need it, boss," he said.

I looked from Daniel to Muxy and then back to Daniel.

"You're welcome to it." I nodded.

"Thanks bosses!"

"While we're at it," I said, "we know we're your bosses, if you must think of it that way, but call us Muxy and Gavin, will you. We don't like being called boss."

"Sure thing, boss," he grinned, and set us all laughing.

"What do you need a raise for anyway?" I asked him. "You been gambling on the horses or something?"

"No Gavin, it's to pay my boy with. My youngest son, Apiau. He's seventeen years old. Just come from Rarotonga; I sent his plane fare last week when I drew my pay on Tuesday instead of Friday. He stays with me in the house and works here. I pay him fifty bucks a week for a start."

“Why don’t we just get his pay out of the tip money, same as you and I do?” I asked him.

“That way you’re his boss,” grinned Daniel. “This way I’m his boss. I like that!” And he lurched off roaring with laughter at the thought of it.

Apiau Kupa turned out to be a quiet good-looking young bloke. Tall and thin with long black hair, and he soon had several young girls hanging around after him all the time. He was a good worker, especially loved driving the tractor, and Daniel praised him to everyone who came there. He was good at praising people, Daniel was. He always spoke to Apiau in Cook Island Maori because Apiau’s English wasn’t the best yet – and also because Daniel liked to show off his bi-linguality in front of the customers.

I don’t think Muxy and I ever discussed the fact that our worker had employed another man, and a member of his own family at that, without consulting either of us. It worked out so well that it was obvious we should have done it before. It took so much weight off me that I occasionally found myself with a bit of spare time on my hands.

Daniel started the practice of taking loads of rubbish free if there was obviously something useful in them. People seemed to like the idea of that and it brought us a lot of extra business. If they couldn’t decide what to do with something that might be valuable but wasn’t worth trying to sell, they’d bring it over to Gundry Road.

Muxy, on the other hand, seemed to have an unspoken arrangement with the Salvation Army. It appeared that any two of them could come into the Double-M any old time they felt like it, gather up as much clothing and books or any other thing that might catch their interest, thank Muxy with tilted heads and misty eyes and stagger out of the joint with as much of our stock as they could carry away.

"What the hell?" I said to Muxy one day when it had happened again right in front of us.

"I've had to ask them not to offer me money, Gav," he explained. "It was just too embarrassing altogether."

"Embarrassing?"

"Well you can't very well go taking money off the Sallies, can you? I feel more like giving them some than taking it off them."

"Don't you dare!" I glared at him.

"Okay, okay," he grinned. "I was only joking."

We settled into a rhythm, Muxy running the Double-M, Daniel and Apiau running the tip, and me running around doing deals and keeping the stock up at the Double-M.

A year elapsed before we knew it. Daniel's wife, big Mamma Metua Kupa, and his twenty-one-year-old daughter, Moeroa Kupa, and his nineteen-year-old son, Tiromi, had all drifted in from Rarotonga and they were paying off their house in McKelvie Street with big hunks of tip money.

Muxy was putting on weight, and with his half-bald head and the glasses he'd had to start using he looked more like the prosperous shopkeeper all the time. Now and again I'd get a line of faulty stuff from a factory that was going to cost them money to dump, and

Muxy'd go a whole week, giving every customer a faulty tin opener, whether they bought anything or not. The next week it'd be a brand new teatowel with Rotorua spelt wrong on it. Then he'd save up all the sewing machines, or bicycle parts, or comics, and have a special on them, which meant simply that that was what he was giving away for practically nothing this week.

How he ever made money I couldn't fathom, nor could anyone else who knew him, and yet he took a hefty wad of it along to the bank a couple of times every week. It must have been the tremendous volume of merchandise that passed through our hands. The Double-M was always busy and Muxy did every disastrous deal personally. Most of the time I was run off my feet keeping him supplied with stock. And as well as that he was taking orders for second-hand items, and I had to keep a lookout in my travels around the city for a long list of crazy stuff I had written on a clipboard in the van. We were getting more involved than either of us had anticipated. I mentioned it to Muxy over steaks at Maxwell's one night.

"Why don't you get someone to give you a hand in the Double-M, Muxy. We could afford it, couldn't we?"

He shook his head. "No Gav. I'm the only one who could run the Double-M the way it is. People have come to expect to deal with me when they come in."

"I believe you," I said. "But it's a hell of a demanding job. Look at the hours you're putting in. And I'm flat-tack all the time, running around finding stuff for you to give away."

"But I like it," he grinned happily. "I wish I'd got into a business of my own years ago, Gav. I like it," he repeated.

“Come to think of it, so do I!” I said. “All the same, I’m going to keep an eye open for ways to ease up on our operation, before I start losing enthusiasm for it.”

“Depends . . .”

“Sure.”

Then one morning I was in the bank, filling in a form for our account to be changed so that either of us could sign cheques without having to bother the other. It had become inconvenient. A girl came and asked me if I could spare the bank manager a few moments. She steered me into his office and the bank manager came straight to the point.

“Look, Mr Midwinter, I’m sorry for taking up your valuable time like this, but we’ve found Mr Muxworthy a little – er – difficult to – er – explain things to, as it were.”

“Don’t worry about it,” I assured him. “He’s like that all the time.”

“Really?”

“Yep, that’s Muxy.”

“How long have you known him?”

“Years. We went to school together. He’s okay most of the time. Why, what’s he done?”

“Nothing, nothing at all. I just wasn’t quite sure whether he was – er – having me on, as it were.”

"No, Muxy wouldn't have you on. It's just the way he is."

"Well thanks for letting me know, Mr Midwinter. Actually I was trying to bring Mr Muxworthy's attention to the advantages of putting some of your cheque-account funds onto fixed-deposit. If you and Mr Muxworthy were to put, say, twenty thousand into our two-year, thirteen percent scheme, your return at the end of . . ."

"Twenty thousand?" I said.

"Well, let's say ten – or even only five thousand would be well worth it to you, as it were."

"How much have we got in our account?" I asked.

He opened a folder on his desk, "thirty-three thousand two hundred and sixty-eight dollars and fifty-six cents," he quoted. "That's not taking into account any cheques that haven't been processed yet, of course," he added.

"Of course," I agreed blankly.

I was staggered. How could I have not known we were making all that money? Why hadn't Muxy told me?

I told the bank manager I'd talk it over with Mr Muxworthy and got out of there and sat in the Dodge to let it soak in. Thirty-three thousand bucks!

I drove round to the Double-M and helped myself to a paper cup of Muxy's free coffee, and watched him trying to give a double-bed mattress to a Maori lady for less than she wanted to pay.

"We get these for practically nothing," he told her conspiratorially. "If you want to spend the other two dollars I can give you one of these rugs as well . . ."

At last I got him on his own. "Did you know we've got thirty-three thousand bucks in the bank?" I said.

"I knew it was twenty thousand a few weeks back," he said. "I meant to mention it to you. It is rather a lot of money, isn't it."

"A lot? – We're rich, Muxy! We're bloody well rich!"

"Yes," he agreed absently as he hurried forward to serve two people who'd come in.

I should have guessed that having a lot of money wouldn't excite Muxy any more than having none of it did.

I wasn't going to let that spoil it for me, though. I'd never had a large amount of money at my mercy before, and, looking back, I can see that my share of it had the life-expectancy of a match. The safety of all that money was further jeopardised by the fact that I was feeling a bit foolish about not having known I was a wealthy man for all those months.

I couldn't wait to start spreading some of it around.

P
M + M
25

SIX

Standard Of Living

It was ridiculous! I admit I was a little carried away at learning I was a man of substance, but the idea of us slogging away as though we were trying to make ends meet, when we were so well off . . . It was ridiculous.

"It's ridiculous!" I said to Muxy when I had him cornered over steaks at the El Matador one night.

"What's ridiculous?"

"Us having all that money in the bank and owning our own rubbish tip and the Double-M, and working so hard. We just don't need the money."

"Oh I wouldn't do it for the money," he said. "It's not work, as far as I'm concerned. I like it."

"But what are we going to do with all that money?" I asked him.

"Why do anything with it? It's been all right where it is so far, hasn't it?"

"Like hell," I said. "That was before I knew it was there! I reckon we ought to immediately raise our standard of living."

"Suits me," shrugged Muxy. "How do you go about raising your standard of living?"

"Well I've been thinking – we ought to move into a better flat for a start. One with a bit of space in it, and a little more modern. I'm sick of pokey little flats. We can afford to spend a hundred dollars a week on a decent place to live. More if we need to!"

"Good idea."

"And we've got to scrap that old Bedford and get a new van," I said. "That van's the lifeline of our whole Double-M operation, and it was off the road two days last week. It's clapped-out."

"A new one?"

"Brand new!"

"We could put it in both our names."

"Sure thing!" I agreed. "Another thing I want is a decent set of wheels. The Dodge won't start half the time now. We should have a good car each, the way we're fixed for money."

"A car each?"

"Why not? Everyone else we know has a car of their own. Even Daniel drives a later model than us. It's ridiculous."

"Couldn't I use the new van?"

"Why not? It's your van."

"That'd do me fine. I like vans. We'll have two sets of wheels!"

We moved into a big modernish flat with a double garage and a view of the harbour, less than half a mile from our old flat. And we shifted our gear in our brand-new Transit van. The new van made a big difference to our whole operation, and made me realise what a hassle I'd been having with the old one.

Then one day I got the old Dodge going and shopped around for a new set of wheels for myself. Eventually I traded her in on a two-door, pillarless, hard-top Chevvy Impala. Dark red, even the upholstery. Nineteen seventy-four. I refused to let myself become nostalgic about parting company with the old Dodge, and this caused me to be a bit critical of the Chev at first. It pretty soon won me over, though, that Chevvy did. It was a damn good car, that. My first automatic too.

Then, when I could get Muxy away from the Double-M, I made us spend a few hundred dollars on new clothes and haircuts, shoes and underwear. Then on Saturday night we cruised into the city in the big red Chevvy Impala, dressed up in our new gear and with thick folds of money in our pockets.

We cruised up-town, then we cruised down-town. Nobody seemed to take any notice of us, so we went into a disco. Too noisy, we couldn't take it. Getting old, I suppose. So we got back into the Chevvy and cruised across town and had an insipid meal at an expensive restaurant. Then we cruised back across town, tried to get into a strip-club but they said they weren't open yet, went to a fancy new bath-house we'd heard about, looked around in there, didn't fancy getting involved and did some more cruising, which took us right past our own flat, so we went in and made a cup of Milo and turned the telly on just in time to catch the mid-evening news on Channel One.

While we hadn't exactly set the city alight, we both enjoyed our new standard of living. It was an adventure – prosperity! It left Muxy indifferent compared to me. He was contented enough anyway, but I felt much more enthusiastic for work, now that I knew it was a success. I had more confidence when I was dealing with people, too, and made some of my smartest deals, even if I do say so myself.

You had to hand it to Daniel Kupa – he actually talked Muxy into giving his daughter, Moeroa, a job at the Double-M. He used the line that they were struggling for money to pay off their house, and she needed work with someone they could trust her with, and Muxy being like one of the family etcetera, etcetera . . . And Muxy fell for it.

"It's difficult with these young girls, Gavin," he informed me. "She's only been here two days and already I feel kind of like a big brother to her. She'll be all right here."

"Sure Muxy."

She was a real good-looker, Moeroa. Short, pert, shy, dark and bossy. And she just loved a bargain. Her English was better than Daniel's much to his consternation. She was twenty-two by this time, and hadn't long finished her training as a dental nurse, which she didn't seem to be interested in doing any more of. She was more wide-awake than Muxy believed.

She soon sussed-out the workings of the Double-M, and proceeded to alter them around, mostly for the better. She took over the jobs she liked and Muxy did the rest. She even sold stuff to customers when they were busy, charged twice as much as Muxy would have, and had customers waiting to do business with her while Muxy stood around with nothing to do. One of Moeroa's smiles could make people forget what they were doing. Everyone agreed she was a great improvement around the place, even Muxy.

I was the first to spring that Muxy was falling for Moeroa, about three months after they'd started working together. He was talking about her too much, and in that way of people who don't care if they get found out. Then Daniel cottoned-on to it, one day when Muxy and Moeroa had just left the tip together in the van.

"You know, Gavin, I wouldn't be surprised if those two – ha, ha, ha!"

"Ha, ha, ha!" I agreed.

Moeroa was the next to discover it and bossed Muxy around more than ever. She liked the idea.

Then Muxy finally woke up to the fact that he was in love. And he lapped it up. He shaved every day, mislaid his spectacles in some unfindable place, wore our best clothes to work and borrowed the Chev all the time and left me with the van.

Next thing I knew Moeroa had started cleaning up our flat twice a week for an extra thirty dollars a week in her already-handsome pay-packet.

I heard one customer telling another one day that Double-M stood for 'Muxy and Moeroa'. I told Muxy about it and he was tickled pink; thought it was a real funny idea. He rushed off and told Moeroa about it, who clouted him one and then went all coy, whatever that was supposed to indicate.

I liked Moeroa. In fact we had quite a bit of fun teasing one another, but there was something about her I couldn't fathom. A kind of hidden part. It might have been just plain shyness, for all I knew, but I did have the impression that Moeroa was going along for the ride and Muxy was doing all the loving. The only thing to do was wait and see, and hope I was wrong.

One night I was watching television and Muxy was pottering around getting ready to go out. He finally presented himself in the lounge, done up like a dog's dinner and obviously wanting to borrow the Chevvy.

"What do you think Moeroa feels about me?" he suddenly asked me.

"I don't know, why?"

"Well do you think she's very fond of me?"

"Could be," I admitted. "Why?"

"Do you think Daniel knows I'm keen on her?"

"He might do," I said. "Why?"

"How do you think he'd take it if I asked him about getting engaged to Moeroa?"

"Muxy," I laughed. "Daniel's known about you and Moeroa for weeks. As for her – go and tell her you're getting engaged and leave the rest of it to her. She'll take care of it. Now get out of here, will you, my favourite telly programme's coming on in a minute. The keys of the Chev are on the sideboard there."

Muxy and Moeroa were officially engaged at a huge Polynesian feast the Kupas laid on for them. There were about a hundred of us there.

In reply to an overwhelming barrage of Maori speeches, Muxy crouched over his seat and croaked some words about thanks for the party and hope everybody has a good time. Moeroa stood up and spoke in both languages about how nice it all was, and that seemed to be all there was to it, except that Daniel was still delivering impromptu speeches when half the guests had eaten, kissed Muxy and Moeroa and gone home. No date was set for the wedding, but Daniel kept embarrassing Muxy something terrible by demanding a grandchild at his earliest possible convenience.

"Look at that!" he exclaimed, patting his beautiful young daughter low down on the stomach. "She's getting old, and nothing in the oven! Boy, you better hurry up and get cracking or it'll be too late!" And he clouted Muxy across the shoulders, spilling orange juice all down the front of my best shirt.

The time came when we realised that the Gundry Road Tip would be filled in less than three months, and what made us realise it was the offer we got for the new half-acre of land we'd created. Seventy thousand dollars – cash, if we wanted it. I must confess that the prospect of having this kind of money caused me great excitement, while it left Muxy only mildly interested.

We decided we'd better have a conference of all concerned to decide what we were going to do when Gundry Road closed down. 'All concerned' turned out to be Muxy and me, Daniel, Moeroa, Apiau and Mamma Metua Kupa, so the meeting was held at their place. And it was quite a meeting. They had the television on with the sound turned down, the radio on full blast, and the Kupas kept digressing into long arguments in Cook Island Maori and forgetting that Muxy and I didn't know what was being said.

Mamma Metua Kupa had to have her say, and several times during the proceedings she delivered impassioned speeches in her native tongue, all of which was translated by her obliging husband as meaning the same thing.

"Nothing," he waved it aside. "That's only woman talk."

Apiau had very little to say. "He's going to miss his tractor," Daniel explained.

Moeroa, clutching at Muxy's arm, informed the assemblage that she had to go wherever Muxy went because he couldn't manage without her.

"What about you, Daniel," I said. "What do you want to do?"

"Buy another tip," he said.

"It might not be all that easy to find one," I pointed out. "We only got into this one by sheer luck."

"I'll find it," said Daniel quickly. "I know how it should be."

"What I want to know," said Muxy, "is where I'm going to get stock for my shop."

"Close it down," said Daniel.

"Close down the Double-M – No way!" said Muxy.

"Shut up!" said Moeroa, and she slapped him across the shoulder.

"The Double-M's no good to us when the tip closes," said Daniel positively. "No supply of cheap stuff to sell. Bigger and better at the new tip. We can sell everything right there. You'll like it, Muxy, I know. It needs all of us to make it work, but I know how it should be."

"Well you've certainly done your homework on it," I observed. "What do we do next?"

"Buy a new tip-site, a bigger one," he said. "We can make a good business out of it. Get rich, plenty of money. I know how it should be," he repeated. "You put up the money; I'll make it good. You'll see!"

"We'll talk it over tonight and let you know, Daniel. Come on Muxy, you'd better come and help me unload those wine casks, I'll need the van later."

That night we talked over Daniel's proposition. We had nothing better to do with ourselves or our money. Muxy was practically married into the Kupa family . . . We decided to put up the money, up to fifty thousand dollars, for a third of the profits each. The Kupas could split the other third whatever way they decided.

Daniel couldn't have been keener. We went along to Muxy's lawyer and got an agreement drawn up, and changed the name of the company to Midwinter Muxworthy-Kupa Associates Limited, which I immediately insisted be pruned to M-M-K Ltd. Daniel had it painted on the doors of the van that afternoon at a cost of forty bucks.

While Muxy sold the last of his stock and surrendered our lease of the Double-M shop, I saw to the winding-up of the Gundry

Road Tip. I had an arrangement with the Ministry of Works for them to dump a few thousand yards of clay (they had to get rid of) on the top of the tip.

I couldn't help grinning at myself the day Muxy and I walked out onto the street with a cheque for seventy thousand dollars in my pocket. Nineteen months before this I'd been sitting in the old Dodge abusing Muxy for chucking our money away on a plain rip-off because he 'felt right' about it.

"What's the joke?" he asked.

"Just thinking about something you said about luck once," I said.

"There's no such thing," he grinned.

"You know, you just might be right about that," I grinned back.

And we slipped into our big red Chevvy Impala automatic, backed away from the curb, and sent her blatting off up Queen Street with the tyres squeaking just enough to let them know it was a V8. How else could two smart operators with seventy thousand bucks in their kick have done it?

We found out later that the crowd who'd bought the land off us sold it again within a month for ninety thousand. When Muxy's lawyer told us this, Muxy and I looked at each other for a moment and then doubled up with laughter. We'd just made a twenty thousand dollar misjudgment and it didn't affect us – we were laughing at the absurdity of it.

Every morning Daniel, Mamma Metua Kupa, and Apiau, departed in the M-M-K Ltd van in search of the new tip-site. And within a fortnight they'd found it. A ten-acre block out at Swanson in the Western Suburbs. A road along one side and a big, wide gully-head across the back of the property. Daniel reckoned there was three year's filling there, more if we could get a permit to burn it.

"That's why we're getting it so cheap," Daniel said.

"How much do they want for it?" I asked him.

"Sixty, boss," he said it quickly.

"Sixty thousand dollars!" I drew it out to its proper length.

"That's right," said Daniel, trying to brush over that part as quickly as possible, "it's a perfect set-up for a tip."

"But couldn't we find something a bit cheaper than that?" I asked. "We only want somewhere to dump stuff."

"No," said Daniel. "We need all this ground. We have to buy this place."

"It's a bit out of town," said Muxy. "Do you think people will come here?"

"They'll come," said Daniel. "You just buy this land and I'll make it good. How it should be."

We bought the land and took our scheme to the appropriate authorities. It took them six months to finally give us their version of what passes for blessings in bureaucratic circles. And in that six months Daniel set up what he reckoned was going to be the perfect inorganic rubbish dump. He got what he wanted in just about everything because he was so much more positive than anyone else. He seemed to know what he was doing, while we were guessing and hoping.

He didn't skimp himself with our money either. He had the garage from the Gundry Road tip taken out to the Swanson place and set up near the gate. Then he had a multi-thousand dollar eight-foot-high netting fence built around the whole property. Then he had a two-hundred-foot-long shed erected along the road boundary, open all along one side, with a wide lean-to roof added to that side. It cost a lot of money, but it was a lot of storage space.

"It might be enough," agreed Daniel.

Moeroa had the telephone and electricity put on and dazzled the supervisor down at the post office into giving us a post office box that just happened to come available while she was talking to him.

Meanwhile Daniel had three floodlights mounted so the area could be lit at night, and the two big signs he'd had painted up could be seen all around:

M-M-K Ltd
INORGANIC REFUSE ONLY $4.00 A LOAD OF ANY SIZE
BRING OR BUY – EVERYONE WELCOME HERE!

Muxy and I had a few chats about the amount of our money Daniel was lavishing on the Boundary Road Tip, but we agreed to let him keep going. And keep going he did. The climax of the whole performance was when he pulled up at Cable-Prices in his old HD Holden station wagon with the entire back rusted out of it, and casually enquired about immediate delivery of a new four-wheel-drive tractor, with Torque-Converter, power steering, every other optional extra they had, and anything else they could find and fit onto it.

It arrived on the back of a truck.

Big and green and the latest thing. Double-acting rams and four-way-bucket on the frontend-loader; custom-built tray on the three-point linkage; hydraulic winch; spotlights (two) front and rear, detachable cab with windscreen wiper, and every tool or substance that could conceivably be required for its maintenance and adornment.

Daniel saw me looking at him while we were unloading it and knew that this time he'd pushed it as far as he was going to without being spoken to. He grinned and winked and nodded his head. "Good machine, eh boss!"

"It better be!" I grinned back at him.

It cost Muxy and I a hundred and sixteen thousand dollars to set up Daniel's 'How It Should Be' rubbish dump. Neither of us had ever expected to get this deeply involved in this or any other business. And the amounts of money we were signing cheques for were unreal to us. Looking back, I think our main concern was about how foolish we were going to look if the thing flopped. It was so big, and we were attracting so much attention. It was making us nervous.

Muxy and Moeroa were away in the van a lot of the time and I liked to hang around Daniel because he was so confident of immediate and imminent success.

We opened the Boundary Road Tip on a Friday morning, to

get the feel of it before the weekend. It was slow at first, the place was big and empty. It picked up a bit the second week, more the third, busy the fourth. We were building up some interesting sidelines. People started hanging around.

After three months Daniel revised his estimate of how long our tipping area would take to fill. Two years.

Muxy had taken over the gate and was contentedly letting people off their tip fees and dispensing bargains under the watchful eye of Moeroa, who'd taken over the running of the office, and who was obeyed by everyone. She liked being the boss as much as Daniel did, so they shared it; they were both boss of the entire operation.

Apiau drove the new tractor from morning till night and became so expert at it that whenever there were people around, some of them would be watching Apiau impassively spinning his tractor around the yard. He ended up getting so good that he could pick up a beer can with the bucket of his loader and drop it into a drum almost without stopping.

Mamma Metua Kupa learned to drive and hurtled everywhere in a rapidly-deteriorating red Mini, loaded to the roof with relatives and gear mostly clothing and kitchen utensils.

She was out at the tip quite a lot, showing her mates around and keeping us over-supplied with food. Daniel didn't approve of women driving cars, especially his woman, and he never set foot in the red Mini from the time Mamma Metua Kupa bought it with his emergency money, till it was eventually towed away to the wrecker's yard.

Me? I just did whatever Daniel and Muxy and Moeroa and

Mamma Metua and Apiau told me to do – a bit of everything. This suited me nicely; I was blatting around Auckland in my big red Impala doing deals half the time, and I can get a kick out of that sort of thing.

By this time we could see why Daniel had set things out the way he had. The long storage-shed faced the tip across the main flat area, about five acres. Under Daniel's entertaining supervision the people dumped their rubbish in long rows between the shed and tip, with plenty of room in between and at each end for manoeuvering trailers and trucks. Dan and Apiau would go along the rows of rubbish with leather gloves, throwing the fill out to one side and any useful stuff that had to go into the shed out the other. Then Apiau would make a run down the row with his tractor and scrape the fill over into the tip. Then he'd go back up the other side of the row, easing the items into his bucket, to take it and roll it out on the floor of the shed to be sorted into the various bays. He carried the fragile things on the richly-carpeted tray of the tractor.

Because we were strictly inorganic we didn't have the seagulls and rats and smell and mud that characterises most rubbish dumps. There was an atmosphere of excitement about the place – it was an outing, nobody knew what they were going to be looking at next. It was interesting to watch the faces.

The merchandise in the rows of junk at M-M-K Ltd was already the best scavenging and browsing value in all Auckland, and it was gaining in variety and value every day.

SEVEN

The Top Of The Heap

Due in no small part to Moeroa keeping Muxy's impetuous generosity under partial control, we were taking more money for stuff he sold at the gate or our new yard than he would ever have taken for the same amount of stock at the old Double-M. When people arrived with their load of rubbish Muxy would stop them at the gate, tilt his head sideways at their load as though he could see right through it, and then wave them through without paying, and without having any idea whether or not they had anything useful on board. Then he'd turn round and grin that grin of his at Moeroa, who'd be standing in the office doorway watching him like a prisoner.

"What was in that load, Muxy?" she'd ask.

"Vacuum cleaner," he'd say. "That solo-mum over in Henderson wants us to save 'em for her. She makes fancy letterboxes out of the cases and sells them at the Bays Markets."

"Letterboxes?"

"Yeah, she paints 'em and covers 'em with that clear fibreglass resin and puts real flowers in it. They must look nice!"

"Well it doesn't look nice, you letting people in here for free all the time. You've only charged one person all day!"

Moeroa even had some tip fee tickets printed and made up into little tear-out booklets of ten each, to try and balance Muxy's open-hearted attitude towards the customers. She had them for sale for two-fifty each for a while, but only a few firms bought them. They were two dollars each for a long time, but no one seemed to be interested. They disappeared in the finish, I've got an idea Muxy gave them away because they disappeared in the same way a lot of our stuff went – you suddenly realise you haven't seen your soldering-iron around for a while, usually just when you need it for something, and it turns out that it's taken its place in the continuous procession of bargains Muxy was gleefully contriving to hand out to our growing clientele.

Daniel had a lucrative sideline. He'd set up a workshop in the back two-thirds of the garage and the only arguments he and Moeroa ever had were about the boundary between Daniel's workshop and Moeroa's office. The first you'd know there would be a rapid outburst of Cook Island Maori from Moeroa. Then Daniel would come in with an authoritative tone in his voice. Then Moeroa would break in shouting, and there'd be a torrent of Maori argument that would rise to a crescendo and end in a mighty crash, as Moeroa picked up the encroaching article of Daniel's hardware and fired it into the back of the shed and shouted at it to stay there. Daniel would find something to do down the yard for a while.

He had everything he needed in his workshop, even a welding outfit, though some of the gear he'd accumulated could only have been recognised by real old-timers, and whenever he wasn't doing anything else he was in the workshop fixing things. I know for a fact that in one week alone he made four hundred dollars from bicycles he'd fixed up and got Moeroa to sell for him.

Scavengers had become respectable at M-M-K, we welcomed

them.

We were all scavengers ourselves, and before long we had a dozen or so regulars as colourful as the rest of the stuff in the yard. There was Freddy, spare and gaunt, always wore a pinstriped suit and rode a bicycle he'd got from us with a basket on the front, a big basket, like the butcher-delivery boys used in the old days. Freddy liked old car name-plates, hub-caps, number-plates, and things. He had the idea that the heap we threw all that kind of stuff into was his own personal pile, and he used to complain to Moeroa whenever he found that someone else had been into his stuff.

"Have they, Freddy?" she'd say with her hands on her hips. "I'll speak to Gavin about that as soon as he gets back from town!"

"They've taken that Buick hub-cap I was saving," he grizzled.

"Well I'll just make a note on the blackboard for them to save you the very next one that comes in."

"Thanks missus." And, the day's business satisfactorily concluded, he wobbled off on his bicycle in the direction of his cottage and garden across in Ranui.

Then there was Nicky, a fussy, well-dressed little chap with a surreptitious way of scavenging, as though you weren't supposed to think he was a dump-digger from way back at all, but there on some other business. He liked to get there early on Saturday mornings and hurry about, waiting for new perks to be dumped, whereupon he'd forget his dignity altogether and dive into it with the best of them.

He was interested in old books and clocks, and very nervous of Apiau on the tractor. He'd be engrossed in searching through a pile of junk when suddenly the tractor would be roaring down on him. Nicky could only cower there and watch as the wheels of the tractor churned past, half an inch from some precious book or flimsy clock he'd carefully placed there. He would wave at Apiau to try and warn him to keep clear, but Apiau was always casually looking at something across the other side of the yard.

Another of our regulars was Slim-the-Aussie. He called everyone 'Digger' and clouted down on most of the army stuff that could be carried away. If it was anything to do with any army, Slim-the-Aussie wanted it. He'd take things that only looked as though they might have something to do with the army, just in case. And he never brought anything back – he must have had a fantastic collection at home.

Muxy sold Slim-the-Aussie the shell and tracks of a brengun-carrier for a dollar seventy-five and told him he could leave it parked by the fence there till he could shift it. He never did, but he sometimes wandered around it and stood in it for a while. A war-victim, Slim-the-Aussie, a bit touched in the swede, but we all liked him, especially Muxy.

One day Slim-the-Aussie told Muxy that he was going to have a big clean-up at home. Put everything in order. And Muxy impulsively offered him Moeroa to help.

"Take Moeroa, she's good at tidying up!" he said. What Muxy didn't know was that Moeroa and I were coming up behind him, and Moeroa had a bundle of rolls of wallpaper in her arms. And she heard what Muxy said. Without pausing in her stride, Moeroa walked up and caught Muxy a terrific biff over the head with the bundle of wallpaper, which burst apart, sending rolls of wallpaper bouncing and rolling in all directions. Still without pausing in her stride she stamped into the office and slammed the door.

“What was all that about?” asked Muxy blankly.

I think she’s trying to tell you that Slim-the-Aussie wouldn’t want a woman hanging around a military operation,” I said.

“Oh!”

That little indiscretion caused Muxy to have to volunteer to help Daniel and Apiau re-block the Kupa’s house.

Two retired Maori ladies came every couple of days, if the weather was fine, and spent a few hours looking around. Mrs Wikato and her sister. They must have refurnished and redecorated their place completely out of our yard. These two old dears had Muxy absolutely conned. They started a kind of special layby arrangement with him, whereby they asked him to let them know what they owed for it next time and took it with them. The only thing they laid-by was the money!

“How much do we owe you for the other day, Muxy?” they’d ask sweetly.

“I’m not quite sure,” he’d say. “I thought we were all square.”

“Oh, well just put us down for what we owe for this pressure-cooker please. We’ll pay on pension day.”

“Okay, Mrs Wikato,” he lied, “I’ll remember!”

“Kia ora!”

Mario the Dally was another old bloke who hung around M-M-K. He always pushed a wheelbarrow with a couple of empty sacks in it. He lived in an old farmhouse on the other side of our tipping gully and came every working day at the same time, just after smoko in the morning. He'd park his wheelbarrow outside the office and stick his big red face in the door and shout at Moeroa, "Got any good leather, Lady?"

"Hullo Mario. You'd better go down to the shed and ask Daniel or Gavin."

"Right-oh, lady. I'll see you on the way back."

"Okay."

"Where's all y' leather?" he'd shout at us.

"There's some in that tea-chest there, Mario. Make sure you put back everything you don't want."

"How much do you want for these two bits?"

"Forget it, you can have that."

"No you don't, young fellah, I always pay cash. Never owed a penny in me life. Don't believe in it."

"Well pay Muxy up at the gate."

"Right-oh."

"Bye Mario."

And Muxy would put a hundred bucks on it and let Mario

beat him down to twenty-five cents.

Then there was Later-Ron, who rattled around in one of those Morris Minor vans and was apparently never on time for anything. He was always trying to make a profit and whenever he found something that looked promising to him he'd try to beat Muxy down for it. But there was a difference between letting Muxy give you a bargain and asking him for one. Moeroa and I heard Later-Ron and Muxy doing a deal one day outside the office.

"Hey Muxy, what's the story on these few lead-head nails here. I've got a bit of loose iron on the roof of my car-shed."

"There's more than half a box of them there," said Muxy. "Why don't you just take a handful?"

"Well, I thought I might just re-nail the whole roof while I'm at it," lied Later-Ron. "I'll give you two bucks for the lot. I've been looking for one of these nail boxes everywhere, so I'll just take it off your hands."

"Lead-head nails are worth more than seven cents each," said Muxy. "You can have these for three cents each. That's less than half what you'd have to pay anywhere else."

"But these aren't new," protested Later-Ron. "They're even starting to go rusty!"

"We sell a lot of rusty stuff here," said Muxy unhelpfully.

"Well how much is your lowest price, Muxy?"

"Three cents each. That's a low price."

A longish pause, then, "I think I might just leave it for the time being, if you don't mind."

"Sure. Just leave them there. We'll take 'em back down to the shed. See you later, Ron."

It was great to hear Muxy get firm with a customer like that, even if it only ever happened when he thought he was being got at.

And so it went. The handymen and do-it-on-the-cheapers came and went in a continuous stream, interspersed with the hundreds of people who came to dump or replenish their supplies of junk. Inventors, innovators and hare-brained schemers came with new ideas and left with newer ones. Two different pairs of blokes were doing business by buying stuff from us and selling it cheap somewhere else. One pair ran a second-hand shop over in Remuera Road, and the other two used to flog it round the second-hand shops and make a buck that way.

They were obviously quite sharp dealers, those blokes, and yet they always shrewdly offered Muxy more money for items than he normally charged for them. They couldn't comprehend that anyone would sell stuff cheaper than they needed to.

I sold all our old car tyres for a buck each, to a bloke who made kids' swings out of them, and filled them with concrete for basketball poles, and a few other ingenious things like swans and plant holders. He had three people working for him and they couldn't keep up with the demand.

We were getting a lot of cardboard, and selling it all to a packaging company. Not long after that deal started we found out it wasn't worth it to us, so we told them we had to double our price, to make them want out of it. But they paid up straight away and we had a good deal all round.

All our scrap-metal – copper, brass, white-metal, lead, old batteries, zinc, bronze, and so on – was thrown into a heap and collected, and paid for, by Tasman Steel. Our scrap-metal alone was worth about two hundred dollars a week.

Every 44-gallon drum we got was pre-sold to that crowd in Rosebank Road for two bucks each, and they sent a truck round to pick them up whenever there was a load, or if they needed some they'd ring up and see what we had there.

All the rag went to one outfit, and the sacks to another. Teachests and wooden boxes were another department with a big turnover. Any one of half a dozen antique-dealers would come at a phone call when we got something they might be interested in. Sometimes they'd get Moeroa to describe the article over the phone and they'd buy it on that and pick it up later. There was stuff with names chalked on it crowding Daniel out of his workshop. Moeroa got her own way, as usual.

Moeroa had a beautiful old silver-scrolled cash register in pounds, shillings and pence. It was in perfect condition, except that the keys were delightfully worn, and she kept it in the office to keep the cash in during the day. The highest offer I heard an antique dealer making her for it was six hundred dollars, but it stayed where it was. Moeroa was probably holding out for a grand!

A big slice of all the scraps of timber we got was taken by a bloke and his wife who made beehives. They took it away, and paid for it, by the truckload. Wood that was no good for anything else was cut up on a saw bench Daniel mickeymoused out of parts. Anyone with an hour to spare could cut up a bit of firewood, a dollar-fifty a bag.

Apiau handled all the bottles and never told anyone how much he was getting for them. He was saving his money to buy a trailbike.

An antiquated steam-cleaner came in and Daniel pounced on it and sweated over it for days, and finally got it working. It was always breaking down, and Daniel was the only one who could ever keep it working properly, but it was handy for cleaning old motors and bits of machinery and such.

Then he got an old industrial paper shredder going, and I got a contract to supply all the shredded paper we could make to an insulation outfit in Dominion Road.

Daniel just happened to know of a relative of his, cousin actually, who was a damn good paper shredding machine operator, and who just happened to be available. He was also, Daniel assured me, a damn good firewood cutter-upper, and we'd been falling behind in that department because nobody liked doing it.

"Sure, Daniel," I said. "We'll give him a go. When can he start?"

"He started this morning, boss," said Daniel grinning. "He reckons he can have three hundredweight of paper shredded by tonight."

"What's his name?"

"Nukutaro – but he gets called Nuke."

"Okay, we'll see how he goes."

Nuke had his three hundredweight of paper shredded by just before lunchtime. He was quiet and industrious, ugly as hell, about fifty or sixty years old, heart of gold, stuck to himself and minded his own business. One of those people who are happy to be left alone. He rode back and forth on a very old 50cc motor scooter.

"Do you think Nuke's happy, Daniel?" Muxy asked him one day when we were having lunch and watching Nuke eat his alone down by the sawbench.

"Yes," said Daniel. "He's very happy, he always looks unhappy, but he's happy all right. He's especially happy these days."

"How come?"

"He's got a job. Nuke likes working, it makes him happy."

"You could have fooled me!" I said. "But good on him, he's a damn good worker, I'll say that for him."

"I told you that," Daniel reminded me.

"So you did," I grinned back at him.

Muxy and I were a bit worried when we found out that Daniel had tendered for a truck and six rubbish skips that were being sold on behalf of a bankrupt company. He wanted to advertise cheap inorganic rubbish collection, and it sounded like a failure to me. We were even more worried when our tender was accepted, but Daniel reckoned there was profit in it and calmly ordered an umpteen-dollar paint job done on the truck and skips. Then he got Moeroa to organise him a few radio commercials and the work started coming in.

One of the first jobs we got with the skips was a complete demolition job. A concrete-and-brick, two-storeyed building in Point Chevalier. I thought we were down the drain that time, but the bricks we got out of it more than covered us, and I managed to get rid of all the concrete for forty-five bucks a load to the County for erosion protection along a section of beach at Herald Island.

Within a month Daniel was ringing up all over the place trying to find more skips. Of course the bin operation necessitated the employment of another relative of Daniel's. Tapo was another cousin of some sort, about forty, not a bad bloke. He did a good job, liked doing it and never bothered anyone else about it. Moeroa slotted the bin business in with the rest of the things she was keeping organised and you had to ask her if you wanted to know how it was going.

Although Moeroa at the office was the centre of the whole operation, it was Daniel who had the idea in the first place, set it up the way he wanted it, made each department independent of the others and yet part of it, and kept it that way while he continued looking around for more to do. Where was the limit? And how many more of his relatives were we going to end up with?

"How many more of these relatives have you got waiting in the wings, Daniel?" I asked him.

"You got the job – I got the relative," he laughed. "That Tapo working all right boss?"

"Sure," I said. "It looks like you Kupas work as well as you breed!"

One day I happened to mention to Daniel that one of the biggest hassles in the rubbish disposal business was car bodies. "If we had one of those gadgets that squash them into a block of scrap-metal we'd have the problem beat," I said.

"There was one advertised in the paper a couple of days ago," he said. "In Australia somewhere. I'll see if I can find it again."

He brought the cutting to work the next day. And four days after that I flew out of Mangere, headed for Melbourne.

I met the blokes at the company that was selling the car crusher and had a great time with them. We had a lot in common, though they were a long way behind Daniel when it came to making a buck out of rubbish. They couldn't give me a demo of the car crusher in action because it takes too much to set them up, but they swore it was in good condition and offered to defer half the payment until the plant was set up and working on our premises at Swanson. I decided to risk it, and accepted the deal.

Transporting all that awkward tonnage of machinery from Melbourne to Swanson took a bit of organising and paying for, but seven weeks after I got back from Aussie we had it there and working. The cost had been a bit sobering, but before we even had it working I'd signed a contract with Tasman Steel for all the compressed car bodies we could supply them with. And we had old car bodies stacked up so far ahead it wasn't worth thinking about.

This project, I suddenly noticed, required the employment and training of yet another Cook Islander.

"That new bloke wouldn't be a relative of yours, by any chance, would he Daniel?"

"Tiromi?" – Funny you should say that, boss. He's my second-youngest son, as well."

"As well as what?"

"As well as being the best damn worker we've got here," he said. "I've been wanting to get hold of Tiromi, but he's been working in the forestry down Tokoroa. He's okay now, he likes that machine."

I had the ridiculous impression just then that Daniel had actually engineered the whole car crusher setup just so he could give another member of his family a job. But of course not.

Tiromi was a good worker, but he was also a bit wild, and a bit unreliable, and a bit of a bad influence on Apiau, I suspected. They got around together on their trail bikes and seemed to have new girlfriends every time you turned around. They preferred pale girls with long blonde hair, my observations informed me. Either that or pale girls with long blonde hair picked Tiromi and Apiau. Tiromi was twenty and Apiau eighteen, and Tiromi was the leader. No complaints about his work, though. He had the Kupa *go* in him!

Now that we were handling car bodies the car wreckers loved us. So did the A.R.A. and the councils and counties and everyone else with old car bodies lying around. They were only too happy to deliver them, pay us three bucks to dump them beside the car crusher, and then go back for another load. While all we had to do was drop them into the crusher and tip them out in eighteen dollar blocks. We had to set aside two acres of ground for just this section of our expanding operation.

By this time there were nine of us more or less working at the yard, and we were getting quite a fleet of vehicles. There was my Chev, Muxy and Moeroa usually used the Transit van, Mamma Metua Kupa, now our official paid tea-lady, still had her red Mini holding together, Tiromi and Apiau had their trail bikes, Nuke had his motor scooter. Tapo used the bin truck for all his running around, even on the weekends – and Daniel still used his old HD Holden station wagon with the whole back rusted out of it. It was a disgraceful wreck.

Daniel was mending a hole in a fishing net he'd strung up between the corner of the office and the fence one day and the rest of us had just knocked off for lunch.

"Can I borrow your car, Daniel?" I asked. "I just want to shift it."

Daniel grunted and I got the thing started and drove it down to where Tiromi was climbing onto his machine. I stepped out of the Holden just as Tiromi's grab buried itself in the windows and roof and swung it up into the air.

"My car!" yelled Daniel. "Put it down. You'll wreck it!" Tiromi couldn't hear him anyway. He dropped the rusty old station wagon into the crusher and jammed it into a block of metal about three feet square and rolled it out into the heap.

"My tools," wailed Daniel. "My lunch – I'll murder that Tiromi!"

Before he got too worked up about it we took him round the back of the office and gave him the keys of the brand new station wagon we'd bought him and transferred his things into, including his lunch. It was a week or so before he saw our point, though.

All in all, M-M-K's inorganic rubbish tip in Boundary Road was doing conspicuously well. So conspicuously well that Muxy's lawyer urged us to let him register the idea of us. A bit too conspicuously well, as it turned out later on.

EIGHT

Tough At The Top

The M-M-K Tip had been going for about nine months when we started coming to the attention of the news media. Firstly, the Channel-One TV people came out and shot an item about our car crushing unit because it was the first thing of its kind in the country. They interviewed Daniel, who suddenly discovered he should have been an actor. He bunged it on something terrible.

There were twelve of us crowded into the lounge at our flat to watch him on our colour telly. He wasn't bad, either, except that he'd have liked them to do it again so he could bung it on even more.

Several newspaper reporters came and did articles about us. One reporter, after talking to Muxy, described us as, 're-distributors of surplus necessities in a depressed economy', whatever that was supposed to mean. Moeroa was featured in a weekly paper handing over a cheque for five hundred dollars to officials, from the proceeds of the Old-folks' Corner Muxy and I had fenced off for people to put their good junk in if they wanted to.

Not long after that a lady from a women's magazine came and did a long interview with Moeroa and Muxy, the end result of which made us all angry. They'd made Muxy and Moeroa out to be a struggling young couple, soon to face the ordeals of a racially-mixed marriage, and having to work in a rubbish dump to try and get the money together.

I was featured in a Sunday paper, standing beside the Chev, as the man-about-town-executive-dustman-type, and I got two letters from young ladies asking me if I was married. Both letters were marked personal, but Moeroa opened them both, by mistake she reckoned, and ribbed me for weeks about it.

Then some wit of a journalist stated in his column that the two most interesting places to visit in Auckland on a Sunday were the Museum of Transport and Technology and the M-M-K tip out at Swanson.

A representative of a typewriter company was photographed buying their first model back from Muxy, who let him have it cheap.

Tiromi and Apiau kept well out of the way when any news media people were around, and Nuke didn't seem to notice them, even when they were taking his photograph or filming him. He just pretended to be even deafer than he was. Daniel was the actor among us. He unashamedly appeared on everything that was going, and gloated over the publicity it brought us.

He was worried about a whole range of junk we were accumulating. We knew that if we left it there someone would eventually come along who wanted it, but it was becoming a matter of space. We had to either sell it or put it over the tip, and Daniel saw this as a challenge.

"We have to tell them it's there!" he announced.

We got Moeroa to get him an advertising agency on the phone, and told them to make us a radio commercial and put it on Radio Pacific three times a day for one week. He found it wasn't quite as simple as that, but they came out and picked around with cameras and notebooks one morning a few days later, and about a week after that they came out with the following advertisement, which they played to the assembled M-M-K staff on a tape recorder.

It opened with a jingle to the tune of, "In an English Country Garden".

'The cheapest of bargains anywhere around
Are at M-M-K at Swanson.
I'll tell you now of some that I've found,
But the rest you can't imagine.
There's rocking chairs and roofing iron,
Furniture of every kind,
Tricycles and tools and a carpet for the floor.
There are wheels, clothes and windows,
Toys, taps and lawnmowers
At M-M-K at Swanson.'

Then the music faded and an announcer with a very cultured voice came on:

'Bring all your inorganic refuse to M-M-K in Boundary Road, Swanson. Four dollars to dump a load of any size. And for the cheapest and quickest inorganic bin collection in Auckland – ring Swanson 966-636 – And don't forget, for fantastic bargains in useful junk – if you can't find it at M-M-K, you'll probably find something better.'

Then the music faded up and played the last half of the jingle again.

I thought it stunk. Muxy thought it was catchy. Moeroa, Tiromi and Apiau all had no comment to make one way or the other. Nuke walked out halfway through the jingle and went back to his paper shredder. Daniel thought it was a work of genius and accepted it on behalf of the company.

We had it played for one week on Radio Pacific, the next week on Radio I, Radio Hauraki the week after that, and so on. And we got so much business we were fully extended keeping up with it. People could see what we were doing, and it was obvious that we weren't ripping anyone off. They liked it, and showed it by their patronage. Some of the stuff they turned up with made it obvious that many of them were looking for an excuse for a visit and a browse.

They came in hundreds, especially in the weekends, and we had to clear about an acre inside the gate just for parking. Nearly everyone brought some junk and took some junk away, and paid a little bit of money to us for making it all possible. A good deal all round.

We were getting a surprising amount of stuff from folding businesses. The assessors would often find themselves with brand new stock they couldn't sell and had to write off. They didn't want to get involved in giving it away, and they couldn't donate it to charity. M-M-K was the perfect set-up for them. We got to know many of the blokes in the liquidation game by their first names.

It was the same with the insurance companies. We got a lot of damaged stuff, too rough to sell and not worth paying a tradesman to fix. It was worth it to us, though. An old Scotsman, a retired engineer called Ian, told us he'd like to have a go at fixing some of the broken stuff Daniel had piled up around the back, sides and front of the office-workshop. We gave him a go, notwithstanding Daniel's indignation at the idea of someone else mucking around in his sacred workshop, though he had become very busy out in the yard.

Ian spent most of the first day tidying up, and in his first week he made a hundred and sixty dollars more than his wages. He was a moody bloke with no sense of humour, but Moeroa preferred him in the workshop to Daniel, who'd been getting on her wick lately. I never saw Ian fail to fix or re-make something once he tackled it. He was good. An old lathe he restored in his spare time was his pride and joy, and the whole workshop had to be remodelled around it.

It was Ian who finally figured out how to get an old office safe open without wrecking it. It had been sitting around for months waiting for someone who knew something about them. We buried it under the floor of the office and used it to keep our money and important papers in.

We'd been in the M-M-K business for about a year when a big anti-waste campaign sprang up around the country. It started when somebody unearthed some figures about waste in one of the government departments.

Someone else came forward with statements about waste in hospitals. Then they came up with the amount of paper wasted nationwide every day – it was hundreds of tons. Then a big glass fiddle involving the breweries was exposed, and so on.

A 'Waste-not Society' was formed, with branches in all the main centres, and they organised a nationwide petition and started lobbying the government to do something about the embarrassing amount of waste that was going on in a world where millions were starving.

All this publicity about waste was no good to us. It was making people too embarrassed to throw anything remotely valuable looking away. Our business started to fall off. And to add insult to injury, M-M-K became identified with the Waste-not Society. One newspaper suggested that we'd actually started the waste-not movement, and it seemed to stick. To our great embarrassment we were suddenly being hailed as the heroes of the anti-waste movement.

We began to get telephone enquiries and letters from people and places we'd never heard of, asking about our operation. Engineers and officials from other centres came to study our set-up. Committees, the same. We even had school parties come to study and do projects on us. M-M-K was mentioned in Parliament, in a speech in which an honorary member of the opposition denounced the government as a 'Pack of Vandals'.

I was asked to speak at Rotary, and I talked about the general misapprehension that we had anything to do with our only enemy, the Waste-not Society. The local newspaper printed nearly all my speech except that neither Muxy or I or Moeroa were happy about the way things were going. Daniel reckoned it was great stuff. He had a strong sense of publicity.

"It doesn't matter what they say, as long as they say something," he quoted. "I think we should get some M-M-K tee-shirts made. Muxy can give them away at the gate."

"Let's give the advertising a rest for a bit, Daniel," I said. "We don't need it that bad anyway."

But a week or so later I was driving through town and suddenly saw that the car in front of me had a bumper sticker on it saying, CHUCK IT AWAY – AT M-M-K!

Muxy's lawyer sold franchise to seven other companies that wanted to start up similar or the same as us in other places. Five thousand dollars each. The money was great, but a ridiculous controversy arose in the press about whether or not we'd actually instigated the Waste-not Movement in order to line our own pockets.

They interviewed everyone except us. Daniel wanted to publish denials in the papers and over the radio, but we stalled him on that. It might have only made things worse than they were.

Around this time I was invited by Channel One to appear on a Current Affairs programme with a Miss Norcross from the Waste-not Society and a representative from the Retailers Federation, a Mr Sail. I put it onto Daniel, who was much more interested in 'appearing' than I was. It was to go out live on Tuesday week after the evening news.

We were all a bit uneasy about the anti-waste thing and the attention it was bringing to us. A lot of people were getting hot about it, one way or the other. Muxy, Moeroa and I watched Daniel's first live television appearance on a monitor at the studio with some concern.

Daniel looked as comfortable as he ever would in the suit and tie we'd made him wear. On one side of him was a smooth looking Mr Sail, and on the other was the slightly-out-of-her-depth Miss Norcross, the National Secretary of the Waste-not Society we'd been hearing so much about but never seen. The interviewer was a young bloke with painted-on hair and a ton of experience. He introduced everyone and got right on with it and it was obvious at once that he was out to get Daniel.

Interviewer: Tell me, Mr Kupa, for a start may I ask you, was your M-M-K Company in any way connected with the formation of the Waste-not Society?

Daniel: (Grinning) No, sir.

Interviewer: (To Miss N) Miss Norcross, how do you think the name of Mr Kupa's recycling company has become associated with that of your Society?

Miss Norcross: I suppose it's because we share the same principles.

Interviewer: And what principles are those?

Miss Norcross: The elimination of waste of all kinds; the education of the population . . .

Daniel: (Interrupting) That's no good to us. If people stop throwing stuff away we go out of business. The more watse, the better for us. We don't want to stop them.

Interviewer: But you do have a considerable reputation as recycling experts, Mr Kupa. Our information is that you have no fewer than nine different recycling departments at M-M-K.

Daniel: I wouldn't say that many.

Interviewer: Let me remind you, Mr Kupa (Reading out). Apart from the actual tip itself, you have a car crushing plant, the first in New Zealand, which your company imported; a tin compressing operation; a paper shredding department; an inorganic rubbish collection business; a firewood sideline, an antique business; a used clothing supply business, and drum, scrap-metal, timber, glass and probably a few other sidelines as well – wouldn't you say that was quite a lot?

Daniel: (Grinning again) Pretty good, eh!

Interviewer: (Giving up on Daniel) Mr Sail, what is the attitude of your organisation towards the Waste-not movement?

Mr Sail: Well naturally anything that discourages people from turning over consumer items affects the retail trade. Our main concern with the Waste-not Society is that it selects areas of protest that bring it the most media sensation.

Miss Norcross: That's not right. We're concerned about waste of all kinds wherever it occurs. But we're especially concerned about waste in government departments, because we feel that they should be setting an example to the whole community.

Mr Sail: We suggest that organic refuse would be a more worthwhile waste to recycle, but the Waste-not Society seems to have been strangely silent on this aspect of room-for-improvement in our rubbish-disposal system.

Daniel: That's right! We could get methane, alcohol, fuels, compost – you'd need a big bank of digesters for a place the size of Auckland, but you'd get your investment back in the first few years. As well as creating a number of jobs, you'd have your . . . (He'd forgotten he was going out on live television to half the homes in the country).

The interviewer managed to interrupt him a few times after that, but the initial meaning had gone out of the interview and Daniel was hard to stop once he got going on rubbish disposal.

By the time the interview finished it was plain to all that M-M-K was nothing more sinister than a bunch of people doing an interesting job making a buck out of it.

That should have been the end of it, but we didn't reckon with perversity of human nature, and within a week I was wondering about Muxy's luck again for the first time in many months.

Moeroa received a visit from two gents from the Department of Inland Revenue. She turned on her most glittering performance to date and sent them away slightly bemused. As soon as they'd gone she rang Muxy's lawyer, who told her to ring an accountant he knew, who told her not to worry, but they'd better get ready for a lengthy hassle with the Tax-man.

Then one of the Sunday papers investigated the Kupas and found out that old Nuke was an overstayer – had been for four years. They kicked up such a row about 'these Pacific Islanders' coming here illegally and making a fortune, that the authorities had no alternative but to deport Nuke back to Rarotonga, in spite of everything we tried. And not before someone had sprayed GO HOME COCONUT! and OVERSTAYERS OUT! across our signs with a can of Day-glow paint.

Daniel replaced Nuke with another cousin of his, Rupe, the day after Nuke left.

One or two of the papers had been suggesting that M-M-K was set up to finance Polynesian immigrants, which we could do nothing but deny, when we got the chance. People like to believe what they like to believe.

Then Tiromi lost his driving licence for two years, excess alcohol, and less than a week later he was caught driving while disqualified. He spent a month in jail and got a five hundred dollar fine. The papers suggested that a member of the M-M-K Polynesian Rubbish Cult had flouted the law of the land.

One day we started getting truck after truck coming in, some of them we'd never seen before.

"What's up?" I said to one of the drivers.

"All the other tips are closed, mate. Industrial strife. This is the only place that's still open."

"You don't say."

I was worried. The strike lasted ten days. What it was about I've forgotten, but we copped a lot of abuse over it. They reckoned we ought to close in sympathy, in spite of us being all self-employed and a family business etcetera. They threatened to picket our yard, and painted BLACK SCABS on the road outside with road marking paint stolen out of our shed.

Daniel and Co took all this racial stuff a lot calmer than Muxy and I did. They were used to it, I suppose. We were shocked, and although we got a lot of support from friends we never knew we had, the whole episode left both of us depressed.

During all this my ex-wife's lawyer advised me that she was

seeking a variation of the maintenance I'd already paid her from the sale of our house.

We were making more money than we'd ever dreamed of, but the guy who said it was tough at the top had sure been there!

Like all those things, the Waste-not movement died away, leaving only a few dedicated officers to keep the name alive, and fewer improvements in the rubbish-disposal scene. Some places were a bit less embarrassed about letting people scavenge in the tips, but they still discouraged it in most of the cities.

Things drifted along more or less normally, with the yard doing busy business all the time. I began to get sick of it. Whenever something reminded me that we were successful businessmen I felt a twinge of disappointment – was this all there was to it? Money? It's just as hard to imagine being poor when you're rich, as it is to imagine being rich when you're poor. Muxy even remarked one day that the more money you have the less real it seems.

The thought of spending the rest of my life in this scene made me shudder. I didn't know what I was looking for in life, but I knew it wasn't this. It was Daniel's scene, he thrived on it. I didn't know about Muxy, he seemed to be immersed in it. If he married Moeroa he'd probably want to stay in it, though they didn't seem any closer to getting married than when they'd started.

I decided to keep a sharp eye on myself for signs of me slipping into a rut. If I was still here a year from now I was going to make a move to get out of it.

I didn't have that long to wait. Muxy came back to the flat

earlier than I'd expected him one night and fidgeted around, turning the telly down in four stages until you could hardly hear it. I was about to point out that the detectives were closing in on the murderer.

"I've got a problem, Gav," he suddenly confessed.

"Moeroa?"

"How did you know?"

"I guessed," I said. "What's the trouble?"

"I can't go through with it, Gav," he blurted.

"You mean you want to break off your engagement?"

"That's right."

"Have you talked it over with Moeroa?"

"No, I haven't had a chance since I made my mind up."

"Are you dead sure?"

"Yes Gav. It would never work out. I don't feel right about it. Never did, really. She's just too bossy. We'd be unhappy nearly all the time."

"Okay, but we'll have to figure out how it's going to affect things at the yard."

"I'm sick of the bloody yard."

"I've been sick of it for weeks!"

"Let's get out!"

"Let's sell out!"

"You're on!" he shouted, and we wound up dancing around the lounge with relief.

"Hang on," I said suddenly.

"What's wrong?"

"How are we going to tell Daniel?"

A sobering thought.

"He might not mind you backing out of marrying Moeroa," I went on. "But I don't know how he's going to take to the idea of us wanting to pull out of the business at the same time. It might look a bit funny to him."

"Let's just leave," suggested Muxy.

"No, we can't do that. Let me think."

"I can't stand this. Let's ring him up right now and tell him!"

"The first thing you've got to do is tell Moeroa the engagement's off, and don't be tactless about it. I'll tell Daniel we want to split from the business. We'll do it in the morning when we get to the yard."

There was only one way to tackle the situation. As soon as we arrived at the yard next morning I waved Muxy in the direction of the office and found Daniel down at the shed.

"We've decided to get out of the business, mate," I told him.

It was the only time I ever saw something fade Daniel's smile. It literally drained off his face.

"You sure, boss?" He hadn't called me that in more than a year.

"Yep. Muxy and I have talked it over and we want to retire out of it."

"Anything us Kupas have done to upset you?" he asked anxiously.

"Hell no," I said. "We've just had enough of it, that's all. You lot can run this outfit better without us around, anyway."

"That's right," he agreed thoughtfully. "Moeroa won't be easy to replace, though."

"That's another thing I've got to tell you. Muxy wants to call the engagement off. It's not going to work out for them, he reckons. He's up at the office telling Moeroa about it right now. I hope she takes it okay."

"Oh, she'll be all right," he said. "If she stays we might . . ."

Just then there was a shrill burst of language from Moeroa in the office, followed by a loud crash. Muxy appeared around the corner looking sheepish and came over to where Daniel and I were leaning on some drums.

"She took it hard, eh?" I commiserated.

"No," he said. "She didn't mind at all. She says she came to the same conclusion a long time ago."

"Then what was all that racket about?"

"Oh, that. Moeroa just finished counting my gate-takings from yesterday."

There had to be a send-off feast for us at the Kupas' house. There were speeches. Mamma Metua Kupa did all the crying and Daniel treated Muxy as though he'd been jilted.

"She'll never get a man now," he consoled him. "She's too old," he said, waving a contemptuous hand at his stunningly beautiful, highly intelligent, very capable, twenty-three-year-old, very bossy daughter, who biffed him one and joined in the laughter.

There had to be another send-off for us down at the yard. They all turned up – there was old Freddy with his basket-on-a-bicycle, complaining about someone having beaten him to a Daimler mudflap; Nicky hovered about like a hummingbird. Slim-the-Aussie saluted smartly and said, "Good luck, chaps!" every now and then.

Mrs Wikato and her sister presented Muxy with a round woven flax mat I'd seen in the shed the day before. Mario the Dally shook hands with everybody, saying, "Right-oh, right-oh! I always pay cash, y'know. Never owed a penny in me life. Don't believe in it!"

There were quite a few others who came and went. Our friends. Of course with Daniel and Moeroa and Rupe, and Tapo and Apiau, and Tiromi, and Mamma Metua Kupa all stalling us, we didn't get away from Auckland until after dark the night we left.

"Well that was some visit to Auckland," I observed when we were settled down on State Highway One with the Chevvy humming north at ninety k's and the tip of Muxy's old surfcaster dipping into my vision every now and then.

"Glad it didn't last any longer," he said. "I was getting restless in the finish there. Business life is worth experiencing, Gav, but it's easy to see how it could gobble you up and make a slave out of you."

"Look who's talking," I joked. "It was you who wanted a rubbish tip in the first place, remember?"

"They're welcome to it now," repeated Muxy, and I knew he was as finished with the rubbish-disposal scene as I was.

It wasn't as easy for me to walk away from a thing as lucrative as M-M-K as it was for Muxy. The money wasn't a consideration with him at all.

Not that we were going to have any money worries for a while. We'd come out of it with $68,000.00 in cash each in our private bank accounts, ten per cent each of M-M-K's profits for five years, and we still owned a third each of the land at Swanson and a third each of the franchise. We were what I'd always understood was 'Comfortably-off'.

NINE

Comfortably Off

While we were hanging around the north and before we found Puha Road, something happened to Muxy I'd been hoping would happen for years. He finally gave up giving money to people. At last he had too much of it to give away. He tried to give a hundred dollars to a First World War Veteran in twenty-dollar bills, and the old boy got suspicious of him and threatened to call the police if Muxy didn't skedaddle and stop pestering him.

Then he was questioned by the police, who brought him round to me to verify his story. He'd been trying to give ten dollars to some young kids. The policeman warned him to cut it out, and pointed out that if he wanted to give money to people who needed it there were plenty of organisations who'd be only too happy to accommodate him.

"I suppose they're right, Gav," he sighed. "It's better to do something for people than give them things. I've always thought that," he added.

The outrageous cheek of him!

There was something about the North that attracted both of us. Muxy liked the easy pace and unhassled attitudes of the people. It made him less flustered and accident-prone. There was something about the hills and the harbour that attracted me. I'd always had a love for the sea, but this was different. There was something about the way the reaches of the Hokianga harbour stretched themselves out among the hills like a flat grey sheet of pewter, with chunky dark dots of islands scattered here and there like thrown dice along the miles and miles of sparsely settled shoreline, and across the headland you could quite often hear the roar of the surf out on the coast. Mounting back from the shore of the harbour the gentle crumple of manuka-spreading ridges rose higher and higher to join the heaping tumble of heavily-bushed ranges back there against the sky.

It was here amid these gentle hills that we found the Puha Road place, and bought it on the spur of the moment. Twenty-seven acres, a whole little bay at the head of one of the reaches of harbour, with a small homestead-type house with a verandah running the full width of the front, which was fifteen yards or so from the water's edge at high tide.

We were right at the end of Puha Road, two wheel tracks of limestone with grass growing up the middle, that wound its way through scrub-covered hills for four and a half k's to the main road.

The only other people living in Puha Road were Charlie Tokai and his family of five kids and an old housekeeper called Mo. The Tokai house was pink and green, with a green and rusty roof, the cowshed was collapsing alongside the road, the whole farm was covered in bullrushes and scrub with grass clearings here and there. They milked a herd of about sixty bony cows.

The first thing we had to do at Puha Road was build Muxy a big fowl-run, something he'd always wanted. Then I set about putting a decent fence around our boundary, while Muxy filled his fowl-run with chooks of every shape and colour he could find. Red ones, black ones, bantams, chinese ones, white ones, speckled – by the time we'd been in the place three months he had thirty fowls and two roosters. He liked the variety of them, he reckoned. Spent hours over at the chooks, messing around and looking at them.

I bought a flounder net to keep myself occupied. I could string it across the inlet outside the house at low tide and clear the fish out of it at the next low tide. I mainly caught flounder, mullet and kahawhai, always something, so we built a smokehouse on the foreshore and smoked all the extra fish. We sold eggs and fish through the store up on the main road and it covered just about half our grocery bill there. We would have been about square, only the cost of feeding all those chooks of Muxy's cancelled out any profit we might have made from them. They were strictly ornamental, economically. I had to admit they were nice to have around, though, and the eggs were very tasty after the battery ones we were used to.

In accordance with some illogical scheme he'd worked out, Muxy paid for all his fowl-mash by cheque and used the money he got from his eggs to buy a second-hand trail bike to go surfcasting on. This, too, was uneconomic. It cost more to set him up for a fishing trip than the odd fish he brought back was ever worth. Except that he loved it. Every time the conditions were anywhere near right Muxy was away out on the beach, the only fisherman as far as you could see in any direction, contentedly engrossed in his favourite thing, surfcasting.

I was keeping my eye open for a small motor-sailer I could keep moored in the bay at Puha Road. Something I could sleep on. I wanted to explore every inlet and mangrovy creek on the whole harbour. It fascinated me.

We found a new type of people lived around the coast in the north. Retired people of all ages. They'd made a bit of money and decided to enjoy it, so they'd retired to their favourite beach.

They didn't seem to like being too close to one another, a few miles is okay, even a beach or two away. Sometimes they'd have mates across on the other coast. They weren't interested in bringing attention to themselves, why should they? They were enjoying the almost exclusive use of natural resources that would be regarded as most desirable anywhere in the world.

There were hundreds of them around the north, you get to be able to recognise them. They usually drive a good medium-priced car and go down to town whenever they feel like it, not very often as a rule. They keep a modest boat and trailer, deep-freeze full of food, a small vegetable garden, a shed full of ropes and tins with oars in the rafters. They have the smooth brown legs of people who wear shorts all year round, and their health is generally better than that of their relatives who remain in the thick of it and come to visit them occasionally.

Their property increases in value every season and their neighbours generally only use their houses for one month in twelve. Some of them retain a business interest or two, but usually decreasingly. Business has to be constantly mothered or it fades away, and these people have made their decisions in that department.

To me these folk were the real hippies. Alternative lifestylers. They paid their bills, worked hard, no protesting or complaining. They used what was available to them and didn't want what they couldn't have.

It was a delight to discover this unsuspected sub-tribe living in our midst and we gradually got to know more of them. Along our strip of coast alone we had a retired doctor, and his wife who was a trained nurse. They looked after any medical matters that didn't require anything elaborate. There was a builder, retired at thirty-two, who enjoyed being consulted about buildings and extensions and leaking roofs and driveways. There was an ex-restaurateur who always took over at barbecues and turned out the best steaks and chops in the north. There was Dale Murray, an alcoholic like me, only too happy to advise anyone on legal matters. He'd been a lawyer.

The retired expert seems always eager to practise his skills as a favour for friends. Keeps his hand in, I suppose. There were also Ray and Cathy, who were suspected of growing pot. They collected driftwood and sent it down to Auckland to be sold by friends. We even had old Henry Blizzard, a retired army man, who liked to drink too much and make a nuisance of himself. He was endured good-humouredly; every group worth its salt has someone like him hanging around.

Quite often we'd get word that it was on at so-and-so's place next Sunday, and if we felt like it on the day we could go along and enjoy a very pleasant afternoon among them. They worked in together and probably lived cheaper than anyone else around. There was always fish (usually me, if it was flounder – I became known as 'The Flounder Man', Muxy was 'eggs') someone often had armfuls of spare vegetables of some sort or other, maybe someone with a few acres has butchered a sheep . . .

They did pretty well for themselves, these middle-aged beach bums. Good friends to each other. Muxy and I joined in occasionally and enjoyed living among the truly 'comfortably off'.

Then of course there were the traditional locals, Maoris mostly. There were a few unprosperous farmers around. Not ambitious, happy to live peacefully. The ones with all the fire in them were down in the cities, involved in the big lolly-scramble.

The old Maori couple who ran our local store were fairly typical. Nathan and Ngaire Parongomai. They hardly ever had what you wanted, or remembered to order it for you. They were slow as hell unless you happened to strike Trixie, their youngest daughter, who was twenty-six and the solo parent of a six-year-old boy called Diesel. She lived with her parents and did all the heavy work around the store because Nathan had a crook back and Ngaire was getting past it.

They'd run out of bread at the store one day and we were just giving up when Trixie came from out the back and slammed a big square load of her home-made bread onto the counter.

"Here," she said. "Rip that into your rotten guts and let's hear you complain about it. That'll be sixty cents, thanks."

We paid her and left with our first loaf of Trixie's bread. It was always the same rich tan-colour, cracking with wheat, and weighty and moist with a nice blend of molasses, Muxy's eggs and home-made yeast. It was, we found, particularly tasty with olives and green peppers and lettuce from the garden, or cold rabbit, or wild duck, pheasant, one of Muxy's chickens – on its own. It was terrific bread, that.

It's funny how when you see someone all the time it takes something – some event – to make you realise when they've changed in some way. The thing that made me realise how different Muxy was these days was one day when I was heading up Puha Road with a bundle of flounder I thought I saw Muxy approaching on his yellow trail bike. He'd gone out that morning and was due back sometime soon. Then I wasn't quite sure whether it was

Muxy after all. Then, as we passed each other I wasn't sure of anything at all. I knew what I thought I saw. I thought I saw Muxy with his pants tucked into his gumboots, big lumpy bandages around each wrist between his gloves and his sleeves, a piece of muttoncloth over the top of his crash-hat and hanging down around his head and shoulders, what looked like the top section of a beehive tied onto the carrier of the bike and a haze of bees swarming around him and trailing back up the road. I turned around and caught him up. It was true. He was bringing a swarm of bees home as though it was a litter of kittens! I made sure all the windows of the car were wound up tight and overtook Muxy, who was travelling quite slowly, and waited at home for him to arrive.

"Muxy!" I yelled from inside the car. "What the hell are you doing with those bees!"

"They've been given to us!" he said, pulling up beside the car in a humming veil of bees. Charlie Tokai – he's told me all about it!"

"All about it?" I yelled dubiously.

"Yeah, it's quite simple once you know what you're doing. But you'd better stay in the car till I get them settled down, Gav," he warned me. "We smoked them before I left but I think it's wearing off. They seem to be getting restless again."

He wasn't kidding. They were buzzing like a power pylon in a high wind. It made me nervous sitting this close to them, you could hear that they were angry and getting angrier every moment.

"Take it easy!" I shouted. "Be careful how you handle them. They could sting you to death!"

"Don't worry, I know what to do. Where shall we put them?"

"As far up the back as you can get them," I called out. "Over by the fence, if you can make it that far. But you be bloody careful now!"

"Okay. Don't worry."

He started his bike and bounced and weaved across the plank over the ditch and up the hill behind the house with his swarm of bees. All I could do was sit in the car and watch, as he got the hive off the bike and fussed around making sure it was set up flat and firm. Then he watched it for a while before coasting back down the hill, without the bees, or even so much as a single sting.

"We can build up an apiary and make our own honey!" he said enthusiastically.

In the old days Muxy would never have got near a swarm of bees without getting stung to hell. I could remember when if there was one bee or wasp or prickle on the whole football field at school, Muxy would immediately, consistently and unerringly stand on it, and the day of the wasps on that beach up north was still a very real memory to me. He was like a different person these days.

I got out of the car to help Muxy get his veil off and within moments I'd been stung on the hand by a half-squashed bee.

"You've got to be careful with bees, Gav," he warned me. "It all depends on your attitude towards them, you know."

"Sure does!"

That's how the honey came to Puha Road.

Looking back, it was probably young Diesel Parongomai who started getting us involved with the family at the store. He had a way of standing, poking his finger into the eye of one of the flounder I'd bought in, toes turned in, his outsize flannel shorts hanging over his scarred knees at the bottom and showing the crack of his bum at the top, the collar of his grubby green shirt sticking up under his ear at one side and tucked under at the other, his nose needing blowing, and his brown eyes looking shyly at you. Kind of pleading.

I had a daughter about the same age as young Diesel and when you've got youngsters you can't be with, you like to give a bit of your time to other people's kids you run into and hope someone else is doing the same for yours. I do anyway. It was school holidays and Diesel had been pulling the same act for a week or more.

"I'm going to put the net out again next tide," I said to him. "You want to come and give me a hand?"

He ran over and grabbed his mother's dress. Two couples, tourists, came into the store as Trixie said, "Go on, then. You'd better go and get your gumboots. And bring a jersey!"

The boy dashed off and Trixie went on, "It's good to see the young bugger getting a bit of male company that isn't using him to try and get into my pants," she laughed. "Now what can I do for you?" she asked, turning to serve the stunned customers.

In the silence that followed Muxy shuffled and blushed his way outside. He couldn't say much about it on the way home because we had young Diesel sitting between us, but I could tell Muxy was shocked by Trixie's tendency to refer to a spade as a bloody great digger.

We dropped Diesel off at the store that evening with a new belt in his pants and a promise that he could come again tomorrow if he was allowed. He was a good young bloke. Didn't know what he could and couldn't do, but once he found out he was keen enough to do it. Always getting in the way and holding up the job because he had to have a go at it, but I didn't mind him. At least he knew how to do what he was told, which is the most important thing with kids around water.

It soon got that when one of us went up to the store we usually brought young Diesel back with us, mainly because young Diesel was usually sitting in the Chev with his flax basket when you came out of the store. Trixie didn't mind him spending so much time with us.

"The bugger mightn't turn out queer after all," she announced to a busload of tourists who'd arrived just as we were leaving one morning.

"Whew," said Muxy as we drove away. "That Trixie sure does lay it on thick, doesn't she!"

"She's a good woman, though," I pointed out.

"I suppose so," he conceded reluctantly.

But he wasn't fooling me, I'd known him for too long not to know that he was going to fall for each eligible brown-skinned woman he met. He was susceptible to them. And this time it was Trixie Parongomai.

Muxy started hanging around up at the store. He had a fairly reasonable excuse for this because he and old Nathan were resurrecting an ancient dinghy that was in one of the sheds up there. They had to shift a lot of junk from it and around it and finally they had it out in the yard. Someone had painted KURI in orange paint on it, which was quite an appropriate name for the thing. It looked like a dog of a boat to me. They were going to 'do it up', but didn't seem to know where to start. They asked me and I told them to start again and build a new boat.

I went up there one day and Muxy and Nathan had an old Seagull outboard motor in a drum of water, trying to get it going. It was one of those things where you wind a piece of rope around the flywheel and pull on it. This one wasn't even trying to start.

"Have you had a look at the spark plug?" I suggested.

After a bit of discussion Nathan shuffled off to look for a spanner.

"This is the caper, Gav," said Muxy enthusiastically. "We'll be able to get out among the big stuff with this! I've always dreamed of having a boat."

"It's a pity you didn't dream of having one in a bit better condition than this," I said, looking into the dinghy.

It had been painted sky-blue, inside and out, a long time ago. The ply was cracked and peeling, the middle seat was a loose piece of buckled board. It had to leak like a sieve. I decided not to dampen Muxy's enthusiasm at this stage. I could step in before he did anything too hazardous, like putting it in the water. They were unlikely to ever get that motor running anyway. They had the carburettor in bits on the table in the store kitchen for two days, and it didn't look as though they were ever going to get it back together, the way they were going.

I was wrong. One day the motor burst into life in a cloud of blue smoke and unmuffled noise. And the day after that Muxy and Diesel arrived down the end of Puha Road with the dinghy and a heap of paraphernalia on Sam Potau's trailer with one tyre almost flat. This was getting serious. I went over.

"You're not actually going to stick this thing in the water, are you Muxy?"

"Yep," he said with great satisfaction. "We've got everything here we need. Can't wait to get out there and hook into 'em!" Give us a hand with the boat, Gav. Nathan's back went on him when we were loading it on. He can't come."

I couldn't reasonably stop him, and I couldn't let him put to sea on his own in this antiquated contraption, especially with young Diesel, even though Diesel could swim better than either of us.

"Does Trixie know we've got Diesel?" I said.

"Yep, she doesn't mind. She just said that if he got drowned he wasn't to come back."

"Okay," I sighed. "Let's put the thing in the water and see how badly it leaks."

We dragged the dinghy off the trailer onto the mud and into the water, where we anchored it with an anchor that would have held a forty-foot trawler. By the time Muxy had thumb-screwed the motor onto the transom the water in the boat was ankle-deep.

"Nathan says it'll tighten up when it's been in the water for a while," explained Muxy.

I made us go across to the house for a brew of tea to let the dinghy tighten up, and when we returned half an hour later the water was almost up to the seats. We bailed it out with a cut-off plastic container and loaded the fishing gear into it. I was slightly comforted to see that we had a pair of oars, even though one of them was almost twice as long as the other. We got in and I pushed us out into deeper water with one of the oars, while Muxy fiddled with the motor.

"There's a knack in operating these old motors," he explained as he carefully adjusted the choke.

To my dismay the motor started and we chugged out of the inlet with Muxy on the outboard, me in the bow, and Diesel bailing in the middle. It began to feel not too bad, but I knew Muxy and couldn't completely relax.

Out in the harbour we anchored at the confluence of two channels and got handlines baited and over the side, and waited for these big fish of Muxy's to strike, taking it in turns to bail out the water. There was no evidence of anything having tightened up, and no evidence of any fish.

"They'll come on when the tide turns," predicted Muxy.

Well the tide turned and Diesel caught a herring and Muxy caught a small eel. I had a couple of nibbles. We decided to shift to another spot, and that's when the trouble started. Muxy got the motor going and I pulled in the anchor. Then the motor stopped and wouldn't start again. I began to get apprehensive. Things don't go wrong around Muxy one at a time.

Muxy pulled on the starter rope until he was getting weak. Nothing. We swapped places so I could have a look at it. I looked into the petrol tank to make sure it had gas and saw straight away what the problem was. The fuel was full of rust. The carburettor would be choked with it. The motor was useless.

"We're going to have to row back," I said resignedly. "It's going to take hours, we might as well get started."

That was when we discovered that we had only one rowlock. I knew it. Here we were, out in the harbour in a leaking dinghy with the tide running out and an offshore wind gusting ten-to-fifteen knots. And one rowlock.

I dropped the anchor to stop us getting carried any further down the harbour while we organised ourselves. Muxy and I sat in the middle of the boat and paddled one each side like a canoe, while Diesel sat in the stern, bailing.

It was a long haul and we made very slow progress against the tide and the wind until we got closer to the mangroves along the shoreline. Then when the water was only waist deep we got out and pulled the boat along towards the Puha Road inlet. The water was only waist deep but the mud was so soft we were sinking up to our chests. Hard work. By this time I would have been happy to let the boat sink and leave the thing there, but it wasn't our boat.

We were exhausted and soaked and covered with mud and cold by the time we dragged the dinghy out onto the beach at the end of Puha Road. I should have known better – I did know better.

All that for a herring and a little eel, but Muxy was unquenchable, and audacious.

"Y' can't beat a day's fishing, Gav," he said, when we were sitting on the verandah in dry clothes with mugs of tea. "There's nothing like it!"

"There's sure nothing like a day's fishing with you, Muxy," I said.

"God doesn't take the time off you that you spend fishing," he said seriously.

"Where did you get that from?" I said.

"Everyone knows that!"

"I don't know that. Who told you?"

"No on, Gav. It's one of those things everyone's supposed to know by heart."

"There must be something wrong with my heart then."

"Oh your heart's all right," he assured me. "It's just that you worry too much to let things happen properly."

"Someone's got to worry," I told him. "Otherwise we'd come undone in no time."

"No, that's not right," he said, as though he was talking to a particularly thick kid. "No one needs to worry. That's a silly thing to do."

It had been a big day and he was getting onto his strand of unarguable, unprovable, irrefutable, illogical logic.

"Shut up, Muxy."

You had to stop him. It gets too exasperating. If you could head him off he'd settle down. Once the bee stopped buzzing in his bonnet he soon returned to abnormal.

We never used that dinghy again. When they pulled it off the trailer up at the store that night the keel of it broke. I had a look at it a couple of days later, the thing was rotten. You could have pulled it apart with your hands. It ended up in the dump, where it belonged.

"No more of your hare-brained capers, Muxy. Next time we listen to me. You're too much of a blimmin' worry."

"You really shouldn't worry so much Gav, it's not good for you. People who worry always . . ."

"Shut up, Muxy!"

That was the end of Muxy's excuse for hanging around Trixie up at the store, but he soon came up with another one. They were having a big clean-up of all the junk that had accumulated in the yard behind the store over the years. The idea was to take the rubbish to the dump on Sam Potau's trailer, but Muxy was the wrong man for the job. Most of the stuff had been chucked out there because it might come in handy some time, and Muxy still saw the value in it.

The first day they loaded the trailer with some tangled wire and a drum of broken glass and some carpet that had gone rotten.

Muxy and Diesel took it to the dump, and came back with a load of corrugated iron that was only rusty at one end and a whole lot of off-cuts of new red linoleum. They arrived down at Puha Road with it. I thought they were on their way to the dump with it, but they started unloading it. I went over to investigate.

"What are you doing?"

"Trixie won't let us put this up at the store," said Muxy. "You wouldn't believe the stuff they chuck out around here, Gav. We didn't have enough room on the trailer!"

"No, Muxy, no!" I said.

"No, what?"

"No setting up a rubbish dump around here, we've been through that one. You can take this back to the dump where it belongs."

"But look at this iron, Gav. We just have to cut the ends off it and it'll last for years!"

"Where? Lying in the grass here?"

"We could build something with it," he suggested. "Maybe a shed to put stuff in."

"No you don't," I said. "It goes back to the dump. And what are all these bits of lino for?"

"We can cover our shelves with it. Makes them easier to keep clean. It's brand new lino that!"

I let him keep some of the lino and make him take the corrugated iron back to the dump, but on the way they stopped for a yarn with Charlie Tokai and he took it off their hands to cover holes in his roof and pigsty. I had to stop him, the idea of Muxy starting up another Gundry Road here made me shudder.

To my knowledge Muxy took several trailer-loads of stuff to the dump from the yard behind the store, but I couldn't for the life of me see where he'd taken it from. He just seemed to have rearranged everything, and it was no tidier than when he'd started.

They were funny to watch, Muxy and Trixie. They'd sit around in the shop, talking and playing cards and drinking tea until a customer came in. Then Muxy would say, "Well, I'd better get on with it," and go out in the yard and sort through some stuff. He'd put something on the trailer and stand looking at it for a while and then take it off again and put it in another pile. When the customers were gone he'd take a set of pram wheels or something into the store to ask Trixie if she wanted to save them, and they'd stay talking and playing cards and drinking tea until the next customer came in.

The junk in the yard behind the store kept Muxy and Trixie together almost every day of their early courtship.

TEN

Next Of Kin

It was romantic. Everyone thought so, except Diesel, who reckoned it was stupid but enjoyed it just the same, because it gave him and me more time together. They didn't say anything romantic that I heard of, but it was romantic the way it happened.

Whenever Muxy and Trixie found themselves together they didn't separate until they had to. Next thing they were getting together on purpose, (a big thing in a small place like this), and not separating until they had to. They'd quite happily walk around in the rain for three hours and come back with two and a half broken mushrooms in their bucket. The next, and final, stage was when they spent all day together and separated only at night when Muxy dropped Trixie off at the store.

"We've decided not to sleep together," Muxy announced to me one night after returning from taking Trixie home to the store.

"Good on you!" was all I could think of to say.

Muxy and Trixie liked looking after the store together whenever Nathan and Ngaire were away at a Hui or Tangi or some other function, because they liked working together. Diesel was spending so much time at Puha Road that I made up a bunk in the spare room for him and he preferred to sleep there rather than up at the store. Although he had to go to the school up the road during the week, he spent all his spare time hanging around with me. We weren't wanted, either of us.

Muxy couldn't be bothered with anyone but Trixie, and she couldn't be bothered with anyone but him. Nathan and Ngaire were getting too old to manage an energetic young chatterbox like Diesel, so it was just him and me most of the time.

Muxy liked the spirit of unity and acceptance he found in the Maori families. They still sang 'Seven Lonely Days' and 'Baby Blue' at their parties and they didn't care who he was or where he came from. If he was 'engaged' to their Trixie, that was okay with them. It was okay with Muxy too. He fair glowed when one of the toddlers called him "Uncle Mucky".

The lovers were away a lot in the Chev, and Diesel and I found ourselves using Muxy's old trail bike to get around on, which Diesel thought was great fun and I was undecided about. Then they started bringing all kinds of livestock back to Puha Road with them.

It started with two muscovy ducks that the owner was going to wring the necks of. Trixie threatened to wring his neck if he did any such thing and they brought them home in a cardboard box. Then they turned up with a white nanny goat with black-and-white twins, given to them by people going to Australia. Then it was a dirty big peacock they bought, for company for the two peahens they'd bought the week before. Then they brought the nine ducks down from the store, because it was easier to feed everything together, or so they said.

Then there were Trixie's two grey cats, Butcher and Blob, they had to be brought down to Puha Road because she was there more than at the store these days. Then there was Diesel's mongrel dog, Tember (born in September), who was impervious to cold, loved the water, and would even retrieve a fish thrown as far as possible into the mangroves. Meanwhile Charlie Tokai gave us a cow with a calf on her, because we had the only paddock around that would keep her in. Fresh milk every day!

With all these birds and animals getting fed on the place the wild birds came around too. Pheasants and quail, under the protection of Trixie, helped themselves to our garden at their whim. Pukekos ate with the ducks, a weka lived with the bantams, and herons, gulls and shags hung about in the estuary for the scraps of fish when we cleaned out the net.

Diesel and I were kept busy for a couple of weeks making pens and fencing off the garden, which we planted half of in maize to keep all these birds fed.

One day Muxy and Trixie left a note on the door saying:
TAKEN THE CAR
BACK LATER.
XX

It stuck. They became known throughout the district as 'The Kisses'. And they didn't care.

Diesel and I swiped the Chevvy one day and were having a look up some of the roads around the harbour when we found the boat I'd been looking for. Propped up on the hard, freshly-painted and with a FOR SALE sign on it. An 18-footer, wide beam, shallow draught, cabin forward with two bunks, plenty of sail and a nice little two-cylinder, water-cooled diesel motor under the stern. It was just what I wanted.

We waited for the bloke to arrive home and give us a demonstration, during which Diesel found his favourite sitting place on the deck beside the mast. The boat was sound. We bought it, and the little dinghy that went with it.

Muxy and Trixie dropped Diesel and I off a few days later and took the car back, while Diesel and I motored the *Inanga* around the harbour to our bay. We passed The Kisses parked up on a headland as we chugged past. We waved out to them and got one lazy flap of the wrist from Trixie. They weren't interested in us.

Diesel got a bit green on it at one stage, but he managed not to let on and I managed not to notice, until we rounded the corner into the calm of our bay and moored her to the buoy we'd placed just off the beach at Puha Road. Diesel was feeling better by the time we'd rowed ashore.

"What do you think of our boat?" I asked him.

"It makes you feel sick," he said a bit dubiously.

"Don't let that worry you," I laughed, ruffling his hair. "You just have to get used to it. It's a good boat, the *Inanga*."

She handled well. Not terribly fast but real easy to sail, steered like a car. Even Diesel could handle her. And when we did run onto a mudbank we could either poke her off with an oar or jump out and lift her away from it.

Muxy and Trixie were welcome to each other now. Diesel and I explored around the harbour for days on end, living on board and growing every day more into harmony with our surroundings. Diesel became the youngest bloke I knew who could read and follow a marine chart. At seven years old he could row us out to the *Inanga*, stow everything in its right place, start the motor or raise the sail, slip the mooring and take us where we'd decided to go, without me having to interfere. We could have lived off fishing if we'd needed to work hard at it. He was shaping up into a fine young bloke, Diesel.

We took Muxy and Trixie for a cruise around the harbour one day and I let Diesel do everything so he could show them how good he was, but they were so busy with one another they were unaware of their surroundings, and Diesel at the helm smiled and rolled his eyes upwards.

"Landlubbers!" his look said.

I smiled and nodded slightly, and just then we went up onto a mudbank and we all had to get out in mud up to our knees and heave the *Inanga* back into the channel. The Kisses slung off at us about that, but we just grinned behind their backs and tacked across into a lively chop on our beam. That fixed them. They couldn't get ashore quick enough.

Diesel and I both enjoyed fishing and cruising around the harbour in the *Inanga*. The fish, the life, the smells, the countryside, the netting of a new spot and lying in our bunks at night, listening to the estuary noises and guessing what was in the net. It would do me for the foreseeable future, this life. I was content here.

Diesel hated going back to Puha Road when we were round the harbour in the boat, because it meant school and jobs around the shop for a whole five days before he could come out fishing with me again. He tried every excuse I'd ever heard before and a whole heap of new ones, to try and keep us out another night and miss a day of school:

We had the date wrong.

It was a public holiday, but we'd forgotten.

They were painting the school.

He'd been expelled.

They were starting the Christmas holidays two weeks early this year.

"The teacher asked me to stay home from school tomorrow, Gav," he said one Sunday afternoon as we were getting ready to motor back to Puha Road. "I forgot to tell you."

"Why?"

"I'm too far ahead of the other kids. I only have to sit around, so she said I might as well not come tomorrow."

"You don't say."

"True! She even said I could stay away all week if I wanted!"

"Get that anchor up. We're going back."

"Aw!"

At various times Diesel tried to get me to write notes to his teacher, Mrs Matiu, saying he'd been:

Struck down with double pneumonia for the rest of the week.

Poisoned from eating rotten seagull's eggs.

Swept out to sea and wouldn't be able to get to school until Wednesday – or probably even Thursday.

Kicked in the head until Friday by a champion racehorse.

Attacked by a school of stingrays while swimming out to save his dog and would be in bed with shock until after the holidays.

One morning he fell suddenly ill and collapsed in convulsions in the cockpit of the boat. He almost (but not quote) had me sucked-in that time. He went to school that day.

I let him get away with it a few times, but I knew his school teacher and couldn't risk laying it on too thick. She was a sharp old bird, Mrs Matiu.

When it decides to rain around here it spills down through the mist as though it's being poured out by someone in a hurry to get rid of it, and with plenty more where that came from. Wet days at Puha Road were real cosy. One of us would drive up to the shop and fetch Trixie (and Diesel, if he wasn't already there), get Diesel to light the open fire and keep it well-fed with fragrant manuka, remind Trixie how terrific those pikelets and blackberry jelly were the other day, make sure the *Inanga* was still swinging on her moorings outside, stick our feet up and watch old movies on our battery-powered black-and-white telly.

Then when the sun came out it would cook the soggy ground until it cracked and popped with growth, and the scent of manuka in flower, and a whiff of pennyroyal and mudflat, and the fantails danced like Japanese puppets in the air around us.

But Muxy and Trixie saw only each other. Even Diesel was getting impatient for them to do something about it.

"Aren't Muxy and Mum ever going to get married?" he asked me one day out on the boat.

"Sure," I said. "Why?"

"They seem to be taking an awful long time."

"Yeah, well that's their business. They'll let us know when they decide."

"Grandma thinks Muxy's scared to ask mum."

"I wouldn't think that was holding them up," I said. "But I'll have a chat with Muxy about it when I get the chance. I'd have thought they'd have been talking of getting married by this time. They were raving on about nothing else a few weeks ago."

"We'd dropped Trixie and Diesel off at the store fairly late one night and I had Muxy on his own in the car on the way home.

"When are you going to do the decent thing and marry that lady?" I asked him.

"Trixie?"

"Yeah, Trixie. Why the hell don't you marry her and get it over and done with?"

"I wouldn't mind," he said.

"You mean you haven't discussed marriage with her?"

"Not exactly in so many words," he confessed.

"What the hell do you two talk about? The weather?"

"No, we used to talk about getting married sometimes. It just hasn't cropped up lately, that's all."

"She's probably waiting for you to ask her," I told him. "They sometimes go a bit quiet on the subject when it gets important to them."

"True?"

"Sure. You'd better chat her up about it. Everyone else around here has been waiting to hear when the wedding is.

"True?"

"True, mate."

He was silent for a bit, and then, "Turn the car round, Gav," he said.

"What's up?" I said, turning into a gateway.

"Turn around," he repeated. "I've got to do something I should have done weeks ago."

"It's a bit late, but okay."

We stopped outside the store again and Muxy crashed and blundered his way through the scatter of empty drums and crates of bottles to the back of the store and knocked on the door. Lights came on. Nathan appeared in his pyjamas and Muxy disappeared inside and the door closed.

I was almost dozing off by the time Trixie let Muxy out the front door of the shop. He had Diesel bundled up in a blanket in his arms.

"Little bastard won't settle down," explained Trixie, tucking the blanket round him on the back seat. "I'll see you guys tomorrow," she said and went inside.

We were halfway home and Muxy still hadn't said anything.

"How did it go?" I asked him.

"How did what go?"

"You didn't ask her, did you," I said. "You chickened out!"

"No, I did ask her."

"What did she say?"

"I'm a bit worried, Gav."

"Why? What did she say?"

"That's the trouble, she didn't say yes, and she didn't say no."

"She means yes," said Diesel sleepily from the back seat. "They talk about when you and her are married all the time at home. It's boring."

"Get away!" said Muxy, hitching himself round to look into the back seat. "What do they say?"

"Grandad and Grandma are going to live on the farm at Matauri Bay and you and Mum are taking over the store as soon as you're married."

"Fair go?"

"Fair go," affirmed Diesel. "They've been all waiting for you to be ready."

"Well I never" said Muxy, looking at me, expecting me to be surprised as well.

"You'd better get on with it," I said.

"I'll ask her again tomorrow," promised Muxy. "I feel right about this Gav!"

"So does everyone else," I told him. "They'll be starting to think you're not all that keen on her after all."

"But I am keen on her," he protested.

"Prove it. Drag her off and marry her."

"I'm going to."

It was the biggest wedding around here for years, according to old Nathan Parongomai. For sure everyone had had plenty of warning that it was coming up, but the way it felt to me was that everyone there was surprised at how many had turned up.

Muxy was nervous and hard to keep still for several days before the event. I had to constantly reassure him that everything was going okay. The suits were ready. We'd paid for the marae, and the minister who was going to tie the knot. Half his jitteriness was probably because he wasn't seeing so much of Trixie, who was busy organising her end of it.

Muxy and I were both properly surprised when Nathan and Ngaire announced that they were retiring to Matauri Bay and leaving the 'young ones' to take over the store.

"And if I catch you giving sweets to them Tokai kids again

I'll have your guts for garters," Trixie fondly warned Muxy.

The day came. This was it. Too late to back out now, Muxy. Yes, you look okay. Come on Diesel, it's time to go.

I was best man. Diesel, all dressed up, accompanied me down the aisle of the little church packed with singing people. Nathan Parongomai gave the bride away. I got the ring off Diesel without dropping it and gave it to Muxy, who got it onto Trixie's finger without dropping it, and they were married.

We filed out of the little church to the sound of the beautiful singing and gathered on the Marae next door for the reception. And what a reception it was! The whole population of the district must have been there. The Meeting-House was filled with men making and listening-to speeches. The eating-house was a flurry of women from six to sixty carrying plates and bottles. A large crowd of mainly young people were thronging around where several pig-hunters were attending to the steaming hangi. The whole place was an extension of their homes; children dashed around in packs, women sat breastfeeding babies, others sat under the trees with little ones asleep in blankets, men leaned on cars and passed bottles of beer. Dogs waiting for the hangi to be opened were chased away from group to group. Three hired buses were parked among the acres of cars in the paddock next door, and horses with four kids on each cantered up and down the road outside the marae, bare heels drumming on ribs.

I spoke to Muxy for a few moments to let him know the Chev was gassed-up and loaded for them when they were ready to get away.

"Thanks Gav," he said absently. "I'd better go and find Trixie. I've hardly seen her since all this started."

As my old mate Muxy walked away from me and disappeared into the crowd I couldn' help being aware that I was the only family he could bring to his wedding. I was strongly aware of Muxy that day, I wasn't even very conscious of Diesel hanging onto my pants pocket in the crowd.

This was more than getting married to Muxy. He was luminous; he'd found the family he'd been looking for all his life. I could tell by the look of him that our walk down the aisle of the little church was the end of something as far as he and I were concerned. It was sad, in a way, but I was more pleased for Muxy than anything else. He was truly happy. It was as though he was being all of a sudden compensated for all the hard knocks he'd taken so cheerfully in the past, all that loneliness.

I watched him blissfully making an appalling speech of thanks, which was enthusiastically applauded by this bewildering array of his brand new relatives. He never did do things by halves, Muxy.

'Not bad,' I thought, 'for a bloke who was standing behind the door when all the good luck was being handed out.'

Mr and Mrs Muxworthy did their best to try and appear interested in the proceedings, but those of us who knew them best could see that they were wanting to get away on their own, as usual.

You could tell by the way she kept brushing invisible fluff off Muxy's shoulder as she wheeled him from group to group that Trixie Muxworthy had everything she wanted in the world.

The hangi was opened and distributed. Toasts were proposed and replied to, and while people from various districts introduced themselves and performed items for the crowd, the Muxworthys 'slipped away'.

They drove past a while later in the Chev and gave up waving before they were past the cheering crowd. They were on their own again at last. No one was even supposed to know where they were going for their honeymoon.

I waited for Diesel to finish his third helping of hangi pork and kumaras and second bottle of Fanta. Then I took him home on Muxy's motorbike. He was staying with me until his mother and Muxy got back and were settled in at the store.

I wasn't much company for Diesel that night, and shunted him off to bed as early as possible. I was thinking about Muxy, on his feet at last! I wondered if Mrs Hollows the landlady would have believed that it had actually happened? It was more than five years since I'd found him in the foyer of that building where he'd caught his hand in the lift doors.

We'd been through a fair bit together since then. Seemed like a lifetime.

The main thing for me was that I'd kept off the booze, and it hadn't been as difficult as I'd feared. I felt I owed Muxy something for that. I hoped I'd been as much use to him. Now he had a family of his own to belong to. I smiled at the idea of Muxy's sons and daughters.

He deserved it, every bit of it, as far as I was concerned. I remembered the way he grinned over a painful injury, the way he impulsively wanted to give people things as soon as he saw them. Getting us into trouble and hoping I wouldn't blow my stack about it this time. Being the five-millionth car across the harbour bridge. The Gundry Road tip – the Double-M – the Kupas, Daniel,

M-M-K Ltd . . .

It had been a good handful of years. No complaints as far as I was concerned. Things would be different now at Puha Road. Muxy had a new next-of-kin.

Four days after they'd left on their honeymoon we were informed through the police that Mr and Mrs Muxworthy, of Puha Road, Northland, had been passengers in a sightseeing aircraft that had crashed in the hills behind Taupo. There were no survivors.

Oh Muxy. The moment I let you out of my sight . . .

One of the toughest things I've ever had to do was tell Diesel his mother and new father weren't coming back. I explained what had happened.

"You're teasing me again," he said accusingly.

We looked at each other for a moment and then he went out and sat in the dinghy on the beach with his dog until I called him in for his bath and mug of Milo.

Next morning he woke me up, as usual, splitting the kindling and stoking up the stove. And for days we just went on with what had to be done, more by momentum than anything else, willing to do what anyone suggested, to save having to think.

Whenever we came across something of 'Theirs' we put it in the spare room and kept the door shut. It stung too much to keep seeing it around. The house at Puha Road became as bare and empty as our feelings.

I don't think I could have managed without the help of the local Maoris. They took care of all the funeral details. All I had to do, they said, was look after Diesel.

Look after him? Hell – I needed him. In fact we made it through the whole ordeal by simply telling each other what to do next.

No one can keep up that kind of grief for long and pretty soon I began to realise that Diesel was taking it better than I was, and he'd lost his mother. Muxy would probably have seen something good in it by this time. Trixie and he were together, which was all they'd wanted anyway.

'Depends how you look at it, Gav.'

'Sure does.'

It was the biggest funeral around here for years, old Nathan Parongomai reckoned. Nearly all the people who'd been to the wedding were there. Muxy's family.

It was unreal, in a way. All his life I'd been his only friend, and here were hundreds of people crying and wailing and genuinely grief-stricken at his graveside. Muxy and Trixie Muxworthy. R.I.P.

The night of the funeral Diesel came and climbed into my bed and had a bit of a cry for a while, then without speaking he went back to his own bed. And that's all he seemed to need to do about it.

The weekend after the funeral, Daniel and Mamma Metua Kupa drove up from Auckland to pay their respects at the graveside and stayed a couple of nights at Puha Road. It was good to see them again and have a yarn with Daniel about rubbish. Took our minds off Muxy and Trixie for a while. The yard hadn't been doing so well since Muxy and I had left. They were still making a living, but the whole thing had levelled off. The car crushing unit was idle half the time, and several of the other sidelines were only just paying for themselves, if that.

But they were all busy and happy enough. Tiromi was back in Rarotonga, digging ditches with his own tractor. Apiau was married to a girl with long blonde hair and they had a three-month-old son. Moeroa, who sent a pleasant letter, was engaged to the new man they had on the gate. A different type altogether from the easy-going Muxy, according to Daniel's description of him.

Suddenly I felt for a moment that both Daniel and I were sitting there wondering if Muxy's extravagant generosity with the customers had had more to do with our astonishing initial success and the excitement it generated than we'd suspected.

Nothing much has changed around Puha Road in the last couple of years. Nathan and Ngaire Parongomai shifted out of the store towards the end of last year. They went over to Matauri Bay. A new couple have got the place now, the Tupunas, a nice old pair. Relations of the Parongomais, I believe.

The locals have decided that Diesel and I should have a housekeeper. They even chose her for us. She's a widow called Polly Mapiu. We've got to like her, though she is inclined to spoil us a bit. And cook! – I swear I'm putting on weight! It's good to have someone to look after the place and feed all the animals when Diesel and I are away on the boat. It looks as though Polly might be moving into the spare bedroom to save having to travel back and forth from her sister's place every day.

I can't see myself moving away from here in the foreseeable future. I seem to be putting roots down, if that's what getting attached to a place means. I just never think of anywhere else I'd rather be. And every time I hear the news on the radio my roots go a little deeper at Puha Road, and I'll maybe go out and dig an extra row of garden or something.

On a summer evening the *Inanga* hangs motionless in the centre of a perfectly-reflected view. Not a ripple – it's so still I can hear Diesel slurping tea out of a mug and munching something bad for his teeth from halfway along the verandah.

Suddenly a school of small fish is leaping across the surface of my picture with a sizzling rush of noise, tearing it to shimmers.

Diesel looks up. "What was that?"

"Stray kahawai, probably," I grunt expertly. "When the moon wanes a bit more we'll throw the net across at Puriri Creek. We could use a good catch, we need the money you know. We're due for a bit of luck."

"Depends how you look at it, Gav," he says absently.

I look sharply across at him. Must be my imagination. I thought for a moment . . .

But I suppose there'll always be things that remind me of Eric Charles Muxworthy.